UNBREAK MY HEART

LAUREN BLAKELY

COPYRIGHT

ALSO BY LAUREN BLAKELY

Big Rock Series

Big Rock

Mister O

Well Hung

Full Package

Joy Ride

Hard Wood

One Love Series dual-POV Standalones

The Sexy One

The Only One

The Hot One

Standalones

The Knocked Up Plan

Most Valuable Playboy

Stud Finder

The Start of Us

Every Second With You

The Seductive Nights Series

First Night (Julia and Clay, prequel novella)

Night After Night (Julia and Clay, book one)

After This Night (Julia and Clay, book two)

One More Night (Julia and Clay, book three)

A Wildly Seductive Night (Julia and Clay novella, book 3.5)

The Joy Delivered Duet

Nights With Him (A standalone novel about Michelle and Jack)

Forbidden Nights (A standalone novel about Nate and Casey)

The Sinful Nights Series

Sweet Sinful Nights

Sinful Desire

Sinful Longing

Sinful Love

The Fighting Fire Series

Burn For Me (Smith and Jamie)

Melt for Him (Megan and Becker)

Consumed By You (Travis and Cara)

The Jewel Series

A two-book sexy contemporary romance series

The Sapphire Affair

The Sapphire Heist

This book is dedicated to Michelle Wolfson, who made all things possible.

1

Andrew

When someone you love dies, there is a grace period during which you can get away with murder. Not literal murder, but pretty much anything else.

Forgot to turn something in? No problem. You have a hall pass.

Lawn unruly? Who cares? The neighbor will trim it, and with a smile.

Haven't returned a call, text, or email in weeks? It's all good.

Driving home while blasting music at window-rattling decibel levels and deciding to run into the silver Nissan that's overhanging your driveway by just one or two inches?

That calls for evaluation. No one's in it, the car is

just parked on the side of the road. I have nothing against this car or against the car's owner.

What I am is tired—tired of everyone being gone, and tired of everything being mine, and tired of life wringing every emotion from me for the last few years.

Besides, when making decisions, my brother always said, *"At the end of my life, when I'm looking back, will I regret not doing this?"* Fine, he was usually talking about traveling to Italy or going to the beach to surf, but I'm pretty sure I'm *not* going to regret hitting this car for no reason whatsoever.

Wait. I don't have *no* reason. I have *every* reason.

I bang into it one, two, three, four, five times, each hit rocking my head back and jump-starting me with paddles that shock my system.

Yes.

That's better.

For a few seconds, I feel a spark inside me, like a match lit in a darkened cave. I try to capture it, to let that flicker ignite into a want or a desire.

But then the flame gutters out, and I'm back to the way I was before.

I shift into reverse, and something makes an annoying scratching sound against the road. I pull into my driveway, get out, then walk around to the front. The fender is dragging on the ground. Looks like the engine might be smoking.

"Whatever."

I don't feel like dealing, because dealing requires too much energy, and energy is what I lack. I grab the mail, head inside, and flop onto the couch.

My dog, Sandy, joins me, curling up with her head on my knee. As I rub Sandy's ears, I wonder briefly if they will send me to anger-management class or something, but there's no *they* to send me away. There's no wife, since there's no woman on the scene. Hell, there's not even anyone to order me around at the law firm I've just inherited. Sure, there's my cousin Kate, and while she's not afraid to kick my butt from time to time, she has her own life. Besides, I'm twenty-five, and I need to take care of my own shit, especially since all the other *they*s are all gone. My brother, Ian, died four weeks ago, my parents passed away seven years ago, and my older sister, Laini, lives thirteen time zones away, which is too many miles to matter.

I put my arms behind my head. What else can I get away with? Is there an expiration date on the pity free pass?

I glance at the empty Three Martians pizza box on the coffee table and pull it toward me with my foot to see if there might still be a slice in it. Sandy watches my foot then the box.

"Sandy, did you finish the pizza?"

She says nothing, just tilts her sleek black head to the side.

"Well, can you call and order another one?"

She puts one of her white paws on my chest.

The phone rings.

"Maybe Three Martians can read our minds." The guy who owns our favorite pizza place includes dog biscuits when I order.

I stretch out my arm to the coffee table, grab the phone, and answer. "I'll take one cheese pie for delivery please, extra mushrooms, and a side of peanut butter dog biscuits."

But it's not Omar. It's Mrs. Callahan from next door.

"Is everything all right?" she asks.

"Everything is fine."

Fine is the ultimate non-committal adjective. If "fine" were a dude, he'd be a bachelor forever.

"Are you sure? Do you need anything?"

I flip through the mail: a hospital bill. Awesome. Those never stop coming. Ooh, another sympathy card. The envelope is light blue, because all sympathy cards must be delivered in the color of the sky. No need to open that. A postcard reminder about the luncheon that follows the dean's reception later this week—a reception Ian had wanted to attend after my law school graduation ceremony that same day.

I toss that postcard away. It crash-lands on white tiles on the other side of the coffee table, where I can't see it anymore.

"Andrew?"

I'd forgotten she asked a question. "I'm all good."

Mrs. Callahan asks more questions about the *car accident* she just witnessed. Not once does she say it was my fault. Not once does she ask if I rammed my car into another car. She tells me she's watered the flowers in the front yard and asks if I need anything else.

Too many things to name.

"Nah," I tell her, and the call ends.

I stare at the phone, and a twinge of guilt threatens to ruin the numbness, but that, too, dissipates quickly, and I decide this get-out-of-jail-free card is nice for getting away with whatever I want.

Thirty minutes later, someone bangs on the door. The persistence of the knocking means it's my cousin, Kate. She's seventeen years older than I am— one of those bossy, know-it-all cousins.

I open the door for her, and her eyes are narrowed, her jaw set hard. I guess my grace period has run out with her. *Oops.*

"I know you hit that car on purpose," she yells.

Who says the cell phone is changing how we communicate? We don't need phones or social media. We have a town crier right here in Santa Monica, and her name is Mrs. Callahan—she must have told Kate.

I shrug. "So?"

"Why did you hit a car on purpose, Andrew?" She parks her hands on her hips, which is amusing, considering Kate's maybe five feet tall, and I'm over six feet. But the muscles in her arms are sick, thanks to a vigorous workout regime at Animal House, a broken-down, un-air-conditioned gym serving a clientele of mostly Arnold Wannabes, guys just out of jail, and badass women you don't want to cross in a dark alley.

I drag a hand through my hair. "It was there, okay?" I walk to the sliding glass door and open it.

Kate follows me, shouting the refrain, "*It was there?*"

Sandy follows too, then noses a purple "Fight Cancer" Frisbee on the grass. I throw it far into the yard, around the edge of the pool. Sandy is like a rocket—she chases it, catches up to it, leaps, and grabs.

This might be the perfect dog.

"So you did hit it on purpose?" she asks, trying again.

"Define *on purpose*."

"Premeditated," she says crisply.

"Yes, then. I did."

"Why? Why would you hit it because it was there?"

"Because . . ." In the silence, every reason I have for hitting the car rings loud and clear. I hit it because I can't hit the universe. I can't hit cancer. I can't hit God or fate or Karma or whoever dealt me this shitty hand.

"Andrew, you're an intelligent man. You're dealing with a lot right now, more than anyone should have to, but let's not go down this road of reckless behavior. Talk to me, talk to my husband, talk to a therapist about how you're feeling. I'm not going to spout off clichés, but talking can be a good thing."

I scoff. "What good is talking going to do?"

"I know it won't bring him back. But it might help you through. Don't take it out on cars."

I snap around. "The car will survive, okay? It's just a car."

She stares at me, firmness in her eyes. "Come down to the gym. Hit a bag. You're always welcome at Animal House. You don't have to work out in the garage."

"I like the garage," I say, and she should know why.

I relent. I really shouldn't be a total asshole. Partial is enough for Kate, given all she's done. "Thanks for the invite, Kate. I'll think about it."

I turn to the dog my brother found at a rescue online. He showed me her picture one day after treatment and said, *"Wouldn't she be a great companion?"*

I throw the purple disk to her again. Sandy leaps, easily clearing three feet on the vertical. "Sweet! Did you see that, Kate? That is one fine dog."

Kate holds out her hands. "What am I supposed to do with you?"

I don't answer. There is no answer. I'm not her responsibility. I'm no one's.

Her voice softens. "Just give me your insurance info. I'll make sure everything is taken care of with the car."

Kate is kind of like a wizard. Give her a shirt with a grease stain from last year, and she'll get it out. Give her a pair of broken eyeglasses, and she'll come back with a new pair, free of charge because she's convinced the store it was owed to her. If I give her my insurance info, I know in a day or two this will all be taken care of. She's the fixer, and she likes it like that. I'm her newest project—her toughest one ever, I'm sure. Especially since she's hurting too. But she never mentions that it's hard for her as well. That she's lost a cousin she loves.

I throw the Frisbee again to Sandy, and then again, and then one more time, and at some point, Kate leaves. She may even hug me, she may even tell me she loves me, she may even say she's sorry that life sucks, but I'm lost in the throwing.

And then I realize I've been out here for hours. Because suddenly Sandy is exhausted. She jumps in the pool and lies down on the first step in the shallow end. I look up at the sun. When did it get so low in the sky? How did it become six in the evening when it was three a few minutes ago? How could my brother be taken away from me?

I walk straight into the pool, cargo shorts, gray T-shirt, flip-flops, and all.

Water sloshes around me. I dunk my head, sinking under, then I come up and tell Sandy all the things I wish were different right now. She knows why I hit the car. She knows why I'm going to call in a favor later. She knows everything.

She listens to every last word.

After all, she's the perfect dog.

* * *

When I go inside, I find a new message on my phone from Holland. Her name makes my skin heat up. She's been out of town for a few days, interviewing for jobs in Seattle and San Francisco. Jobs I selfishly hope she doesn't get, so she won't have to leave yet again.

Holland: How are you? I'm flying back to LA tomorrow night! Are you ready for the reception later this week? Do you want me to bring you a slice of pie? If you need a haircut, I'm good with scissors. ☺

Just like that, I feel so much more than I felt when I

hit the car—a flicker in my chest, a rushing of my blood, like there's something I want.

Or really, *someone*.

My thumb hovers over a folder on my phone, then I open it, clicking to a picture from three years ago. A shot of Holland, her blonde hair whipping against her face as we walked along the ocean one morning. She looked so gorgeous I had to take it and keep it.

I can't throw out a picture like this.

Trouble is, I can't seem to stop looking at it either.

2

Andrew

The next night, Jeremy is shooting aliens on the TV screen, Ethan is trying to convince Piper that an earthquake of 9.0 magnitude will hit Los Angeles in the next 365 days, and some of the women from my law school are destroying some of the guys in pool volleyball. The dudes are in the deep end on the other side of the net, getting clobbered by the bikini-clad athletes.

I'm waiting for a delivery.

I check my phone.

Trina's text says she'll be here soon.

Even her text message looks reluctant, but that's okay. She said yes when I called in the favor last night.

I tap a reply: *You're a good woman for doing this.*

As I wait, I turn up the volume on the sound system because Retractable Eyes is up next on the playlist, and this band is awesome. But before the opening chords sound, I hear the beginning of "New York, New York."

On. The. Piano.

I turn to the living room, and the aliens must have extinguished Jeremy because now he's leaning over the piano and thinking he's Frank Sinatra.

"Dude, don't touch that." I walk over and stand next to the keys.

"Just let me play this one song."

I shake my head. He knows this is my *one* rule. "Don't."

He pounds out more notes, and he's about to hit the chorus, and I'm not okay with this on so many levels because this is my brother's piano. He fancied himself a regular John Legend.

"I've got game when it comes to the ivories," Ian would say, then launch into "All of Me." I swear the dude got laid to that song more than the singer did.

Well, *maybe*. Legend can pull.

"Jer. Off."

Something in my voice stops him, so he backs away and holds up his hands. "Sorry, bud."

"Go play air guitar if you want to play something," I say, easing up a bit on my friend.

He laughs then stares longingly at the keys. "I

wish you'd let me take this off your hands. You know you're never going to use it."

"It's not about using it."

"Exactly. So let me help you. There's so much you need to get rid of." He flaps his arms, gesturing to the whole damn house.

Mine.

This house I grew up in is all mine.

The home that our parents owned outright, that became ours years ago, is suddenly mine, courtesy of a heart that no longer beats and a sister who didn't want a thing. Everything under this roof is mine, and all of it weighs ten thousand tons.

Like Ian's clothes. His law school tomes. His desk. Yes, even his piano. And, of course, his baseball cards. *"Someday this fortune will be yours,"* he'd joke while flipping through cards—some worth something, some worth nothing, but all worth everything to a fanatic like him. I couldn't look at those boxes, so I shoved them into the hall closet the other day.

"Yeah, I know I need to get rid of everything. Maybe next time you want me to interact with people, you should convince me to have a personal-effects party. We could gather around the boxes, sort through them all, and pick and choose the keepers and what goes to Goodwill," I say drily. "You want the signed Clayton Kershaw jersey, or should we see if Ethan calls dibs?"

Jeremy sighs. "Shit, man. Sorry." He gestures to

the pool, where nearly everyone has gathered. "I thought it would be helpful."

Jeremy wanted to throw this party. He said it was what I needed. *"Gotta keep things normal, man. Keep going. Keep talking. Hang out with people. Let us be there for you."* I agreed because I should be studying for the Bar, and anything's better than that.

I clap his back. "It's fine. You can have the jersey."

"It's okay. Don't worry about it. You keep it."

"I mean it. I'll track it down for you." I nod to the pool. "Now go. Have some fucking fun."

"You're not pissed off?"

I laugh, but it's mirthless. "I wish I were pissed off."

Pissed off at least would feel like something.

Jeremy heads to the pool, and I survey the scene in my yard, trying, trying so hard for a contact high as I watch my friend jump into the pool and smack a volleyball at a girl in a yellow bikini.

I love pool volleyball. I should be out there.

"You could join them." I turn around to see Trina has arrived.

"The woman of the hour." I hold out my arms and flash her a big, practiced grin.

She shakes her head. "Andrew."

"C'mon. You love me. That's why you're here."

She rolls her brown eyes. "You're not making this any easier." She tips her chin to the party. "That's what you should be doing."

I press my hands together, turning myself into a beggar. "Yes, and I will. But for now, I could use a snack."

My brother's good friend—one of his closest friends—dips her hand into her pocket and glances around the living room as if sweeping the home for spies.

She takes out a Ziploc bag and presses it into my palm. "This is all I had handy at the hospital, and I could lose my job, so don't say a word."

"I'm a vault, Trina."

"People say that . . ."

"But it's true in this case. Only the dog knows my secrets, and she doesn't talk."

"Let's keep it that way."

I mime zipping my lips. "I'll administer them sparingly."

She narrows her eyes. "You better. I swear."

Trina has been friends with my brother since they went to high school together. Since she helped him in science, and he helped her in history. Now, she has an MD and a soft spot when it comes to the dead's younger brother.

Lucky me.

She heads to the kitchen, pours a glass of water, and thrusts it in my hand. "Just take half. I already split them."

"Bless you and your pill-cutting skills."

I fish around in the bag and find half a tablet. I swallow it, chasing it with water.

"I'm a good boy. I took all my medicine," I say, but she doesn't laugh.

She shakes her head. "Your brother would kill me."

"He would understand. Trust me." I'd hit his stash, but it's long gone. Kate cleaned up quickly. That was the only thing she cleaned up quickly. All the other shit is up to me.

I gaze out at the pool, a sea of glistening flesh and fun. The problem is there's no secondhand high from my friends. But maybe, just maybe, a welcome pharmaceutical haze will kick in shortly and . . . help me fake happiness.

"I need to go," Trina says, with a reluctant smile.

"I love you madly. You know that?"

She laughs, shaking her head. "You don't love me. You love my degree."

I walk her to the door and open it. "Drive safely, okay?"

That's easier than saying other things. Like, *I hope you don't lose your job* and *Thank you from the bottom of my cold heart*. I hope it conveys my meaning as best it can.

She nods. "Bye, Andrew. Feel better."

I wait till she's inside her beater car, a ten-year-old Honda she hasn't replaced yet since med school loans are sky-high, and once she's gone, I turn around.

I could join the party.

I could jump in the pool.

I could crash a car, smash a model airplane, leave a restaurant without paying.

I've done all those, so tonight I choose something new.

I go up the stairs. I hear the noises from outside, the splashing and the laughing, the sounds of cans opening and voices rising in the celebratory din of the end of an era for most of us, as we nab our JDs and MBAs and finish our MDs, and then the sounds fade when I close my door, crank up some tunes, and tug off my T-shirt.

The room's feeling fuzzy and warm, just the way I like it, because Dr. Trina's goodies are kicking in.

I flop down on my bed, toss the goodie bag on the nightstand, and ask sleep to come visit me.

But sleep doesn't come.

I close my eyes and see Holland, the woman who's been back in town for the last several weeks.

I was supposed to forget her when she moved halfway around the world three years ago. I was supposed to let her slip from my mind.

I mostly did.

But then she returned, and the first day I saw her again, reading a book about Sandy Koufax to a too-skinny Ian since he was too tired to turn the pages, my heart tried to claw its way out of my chest and fling itself at her.

Now, courtesy of a text asking me if I want pie and a haircut, I'm replaying our greatest hits, as I have a thousand times since she returned a month ago. Mornings at the beach, afternoons in the pool, nights tangled up together. One perfect summer.

That was the deal. We both knew the score.

We went in with eyes wide open, with promises not to fall in love.

And we did it anyway.

Then we split, and she started to fade to black-and-white in my memories.

Now, she's in technicolor again, and I love it, and I hate it, and I love it.

Her wavy blonde hair, her sky-blue eyes, her lips tasting like strawberry. Her smell—all pure, perfect, blonde California girl. Her laughter, throaty and rich. Her smile, radiant and a little sneaky too, like she knows all your secrets. Hell, she knew mine. She knew one nip on my ear, a hand around my waist, and I'd be ready. I was so fucking easy.

We were twenty-two then. All we wanted was each other. Images of her flick before my eyes—her skin, her lips, the curves of her body—but I don't feel like jacking off.

Even that requires too much effort.

I watch the movie of her and imagine she's riding

me, her hands linked with mine, her hair tickling my face.

That's nice. Yeah, that's *something*.

My pulse beats faster, and it feels fantastic like this with imaginary Holland. Like I'm alive again, like I'm real again, like the earth is rotating around the sun again.

I'm aroused, and I'm half tempted to take care of this, but only half.

But that's one of the things no one teaches you about grief—it can wear you down so much you don't have the energy to jerk off.

When I wake in the middle of the night, my dog is wedged against me, the noises from the pool are gone, and all my memories of Holland are blurry once more.

The Ziploc bag of a half dozen Vicodin sits on my nightstand. I'll really need to dole them out carefully if I'm going to get through this endless summer.

3

Holland

The day I finished nursing school a year ago, I went to the discount store and picked up a new set of fitted sheets.

Do I know how to party or what?

But the store was having a kickass sale, and the bedding was 75 percent off. I had a small apartment to furnish, and by small, I mean the size of a drawer.

The next day, I started my first job.

The end of grad school wasn't a big deal to me or to my family. But as I walk along the beach at dawn, listening to the churning surf, I picture Andrew getting ready for the dean's reception all alone in his empty home. I imagine the echo he must hear as he walks from room to room, how the silence must hurt.

A simple moment, like getting ready for an event, is no longer easy for the guy I once loved madly. He doesn't have the luxury of shopping for sheets like it's the only thing that matters.

I'd do nearly anything to make sure sheet shopping, or errand running, was his top priority. My chest squeezes, since I can't do that. I can't do *anything* to take away his pain.

A pelican circles overhead, scanning the unforgiving Pacific Ocean for breakfast. Once he spots his prey, he executes a glorious dive bomb, spearing an unsuspecting fish in his big, purse-like bill.

A twinge of envy pierces my chest unexpectedly, and I stop in my tracks in the sand. I'm jealous of a pelican?

In some weird way, I suppose I am. The pelican knows what it wants and the pelican goes for it. Me? I have all kinds of stuff to sort out, but most of it isn't even *my* stuff.

Most of it involves waiting.

I've never been particularly good at waiting. I'm a doer, but I've had to learn that sometimes you have no choice – you have to wait.

For results. For answers. For the next thing to happen, even if you have no clue what the next thing might be.

Maybe even especially when you don't know.

I desperately want to tell Andrew I may be leaving again soon. I want to ask him what he thinks of my plans. When my first job ended last month and I chose to return to California to care for Ian through his final days, my trip was open-ended. Since then, I've been looking for work anywhere and every-where, including here. But the job I've found that suits me best is on another continent. Like a magnet, I'm drawn to the other side of the world.

If it happens, I'll have to tell Andrew, no matter how hard it'll be to say.

Right now though, I don't think he's ready to hear the details. Not when his eyes light up when I knock on his door. Not when he smiles when I bring him Chinese takeout.

He thinks I don't know he misses us.

But I know.

And I miss us too, even after three years apart.

I miss us desperately.

That's why I haven't told him. Because I'm not ready to say goodbye either.

* * *

After the waves have done their job clearing my mind, I head to Andrew's home, bracing myself for today's act of restraint when I see him. Is it wrong that I thought about kissing him after his brother's memorial service last month?

Yes, it's so wrong.

But even so, I wanted to kiss the breath out of my

former summer love when I found him alone on a bench, sunglasses on, staring at the sea. I sat with him, quietly.

I took his hand in mine, and our fingers linked together.

He met my gaze, his brown eyes brimming with sadness.

Sadness came over me too, but so did a potent desire to kiss him hard, to take on all his pain. I could do that for him. I'm strong, and I'm tough, and I could bear his burdens.

I want to take everything on for him – it's my instinct, it's my gut.

But that'd be the riskiest thing I could do.

4

Andrew

I have a front-row view of the tossing of caps and hugging of professors right here on Instagram. Look at all those smiling faces, happily celebrating and hashtagging the hell out of it.

I crush the can of Diet Coke in my hand and chuck it in the recycling bin as I scroll through the social media feeds of the law school graduation I'm not attending.

No one's making me go.

No one really can.

Ian's not here to give me that sharp, brotherly stare. *"C'mon. Get a tie and get your ass to the dean's reception now. I told you—the luncheon has the best shrimp cocktail in the free world."*

But hey, that's what he'd say, so I head upstairs and find my lawyer costume, showing the tie options to Sandy. "Green with stripes or red?"

She doesn't bark from her post on the tiled floor.

"Neither? Okay, I get it. Red is too much of a power-douche statement. That's what you're saying, right? Don't be a power-douche."

She jerks her gaze to the window. A bird chirps outside.

I grab a light-blue tie with . . . cartoon giraffes on it? "Why do I have this?"

She cocks her head as I hang up that one. "Did you buy it for me?"

She drops her chin to the floor. Guilty as charged.

I find a navy-blue tie. "There. I'll blend in. It's perfect, right?"

Her tail thumps.

I button a shirt and drape the tie around my neck.

I hold my arms out wide. "You'd totally hire me if you needed someone to make your case, right? Of course you would. You'd want a pit bull for a lawyer." I play-growl at my brother's dog.

She play-growls back.

My doorbell rings, and Sandy erupts into a flurry of barks then rushes downstairs. I follow her, picking up the pace, feeling *something*. Her excitement is infectious. I don't bark, but if I had a tail, I'd wag it when I peer through the peephole and see who's here. *Holland.*

The gears whir to life. The cogs in the machine start turning.

I open the door, and she sports a most mischievous grin.

"The first rule of Pie Club is—"

I smile. "Don't tell anyone about Pie Club."

She brings a white box from behind her back then hands it to me. "Rum chiffon."

I laugh. It's the first time I've laughed in days. "I didn't even know rum chiffon pie was a thing."

"Totally a thing. And a better thing than prune chiffon pie. Did you know the One and Only Pie Shop makes prune chiffon?" She crinkles her nose.

"On the scale of retro pies I find acceptable, that'd be a zero."

"I know," she says, then taps her fingernail against the cardboard. "But rum has to be tasty."

"Should I get drunk on it before the speech at the reception?"

"All speeches are best delivered intoxicated," she says, then eyes the home behind me. She knows it well, not only from the summer we spent together, but from the years we were friends before we were anything else.

"Come in." I take the pie and head to the kitchen.

"I saw you have a rental car in the driveway. Where's yours?"

"It's kind of a funny story," I deadpan. Then I give her the barest overview of the other day.

She blows out a long stream of air. "Then it's a damn good thing I brought pie."

That's another reason why this woman owns prime real estate in my mind—she doesn't judge me.

"I promise not to smash the pie." I grab two forks and set them next to the box of pie.

She taps me on the shoulder. I turn around, surprised to see her inches away. "Hey."

My heart speeds up. I wish she wouldn't *hey* me. I wish she'd *hey* me all day long. "Hey."

Then, the slow-mo begins. She opens her arms, steps closer, wraps those toned, strong limbs around me.

I sigh louder than I should.

I want to bury my face in that blonde hair and get lost for the day, for the week, for the summer. She's so warm, and I don't want to let her go. Not when her embrace feels like the solution to world peace. To my peace.

She whispers against my shoulder, "How are you doing today?"

"Fine. I didn't go to the ceremony." I hum a little as I sneak an inhale of her shampoo. Citrusy, like the rest of her.

"I know."

"I watched it on social media."

"Do you wish you'd gone?" She lets her arms drop, and we separate.

I shake my head. "Hell, no."

"Do you want company at the dean's reception?"

So much.

"Nah, I'll be okay," I lie. I can't keep sucking up all her sympathy. Kate offered to attend too, and I turned her down. Why make it a bigger deal than it is? It's a stupid reception I was going to attend with Ian.

Now, I'm going solo.

"Are you sure?" Holland stares at me like she can extract the truth with her big eyes.

I could take her up on it, but I'd spend the whole time thinking about her naked.

"Thanks. But I'll manage. How hard can it be, right? Say a few words, eat some shrimp and salad, and then I'll be back here, lounging poolside with a piña colada," I say with a casual shrug, like I can handle this. No problem.

"Piña coladas are always a good idea." She glances around, and I try to see my home through her eyes. Undisturbed. I cleaned up everything from the party last night, and nothing else has changed from when she was here a month ago, helping my brother through the end as his de facto hospice nurse.

Back then, it was Kate, Trina, Jeremy, Holland, and Omar from Three Martians Pizza, delivering food and chatting with Ian about the Dodgers' prospects so far this season.

Now, it's only Holland and me, alone in the house.

I could pull the blinds and watch movies on the couch with her all day. We could hole up here and never leave, just Holland and the dog and me. Order Chinese takeout from Captain Wong's around the corner for every meal, and have them grab some kibble for Sandy.

But I remember some of my brother's last words about Holland. *"I know you want her back. But take your time. If you go for it now, you'll lose her again."*

Thanks a lot, Ian, for that fantastic parting shot.

I brandish the fork as I wiggle an eyebrow. "So it's retro Pie Club time, is it?"

Holland presses a finger to her lips. "Shh. Don't tell anyone."

That was one of our things when we dated three years ago: a deep and abiding love of pie. We'd sneak off to bakeries, order the most absurd flavors, then pretend it was a top-secret mission. One day, we discovered the One and Only Pie Shop and its retro menu—pudding cheesecake, pineapple dream, peanut pie.

I eat a forkful and wince. "This pie sucks toenails."

"Eww." She laughs and takes a bite. Her lips curl. "Toenails and old socks."

"You win. You grossed me out."

She holds up a hand to high-five. I smack back.

"We could chuck it onto the neighbor's roof," she offers, since that's what we used to do with sandwiches we didn't finish, with old bread growing moldy, and with apple slices we no longer wanted. We'd sit by the pool and toss food onto the neighbor's roof that hung over the edge of my yard.

"The squirrels in the hood loved us."

"I bet they built a shrine to us."

"Dude, they still talk about us."

I laugh, and when the laughter fades, the memories sharpen from that summer. Ian was well then. Cancer hadn't struck yet. I'd finished college and hadn't started law school. Holland was going to head to Japan for nursing school.

It was just us, camping out in my home, having the time of our lives.

I can hear the echo of who we were then, and I want to catch it and keep it, only I don't know how to hold on to something so good.

Holland stares at my hair. "Do you want a haircut?"

"Do you think it's too long?"

She leans in closer. Her fingers brush my face. My heart pounds a tick louder at her touch. "Some guys like long hair."

"Do you like long hair?" I can't even remember how she likes my hair.

"I like it short."

"Cut it, then," I say, my throat drier than the Gobi.

Five minutes later, I'm perched on a kitchen stool, dress shirt off, T-shirt on. A towel hangs over my shoulders, and she's snipping the ends of my hair.

Hello, nice view.

Good to see you again, breasts.

Yes, let's spend the day together. Let's never leave. Stay here and be my Vicodin.

She moves in closer, her thighs brushing against my knees, her arms near my face, her smell drifting into my nose.

Lemon sugar.

I want to breathe her in and let the day fold like a house of cards. I want to nuzzle Holland and curl up with her, and fuck her, and kiss her, and—

"Do you miss him today?"

I snap out of my daydream.

"Every day," I say instantly, relieved that someone has asked, that someone wants to know.

She lines up the scissors. "Does it bother you that I asked?"

"You're the only one who does. Everyone else tiptoes around me like they think I might break. The other lawyers at his firm, the professors—even the dean. No one wants to say it. Like they might catch it."

She scoffs. "That's crazy."

"I know." I clear my throat. "I was listening to the

Dodgers game yesterday when I was working out before the party."

She offers a smile. "Bet that made you think of him. How he used to shout at the radio during a pitching change."

I laugh. "Ian was convinced he could run the bullpen better."

"No doubt. He wouldn't have lost the World Series for us last year."

I smile, thinking of the games I went to with her that summer, the way we cheered from the third-base line, the way she booed at all the bad calls. "We'd have the trophy for sure."

She finishes my hair. "Beautiful."

"So are you," I blurt, and then I blink and push away from the stool. I hold up my hands. "Sorry."

"It's okay," she says softly.

I back up, walking toward the sink, my ass hitting the edge of the counter. "I didn't mean to say that."

She narrows her brow, as if she's trying to figure me out. "It didn't upset me, Andrew."

But it's not who we are anymore.

I grab my shirt and point to the door. "I should go to the reception. My Lyft will be here soon. Thanks for the haircut and the pie that tasted like toenails."

And then I want to punch myself for the look of sadness I put on her face. *Ass.*

* * *

I walk to the podium, take out my index cards, and look at my graduating classmates, my professors, and my friends.

I've been asked to speak because I kick unholy ass when it comes to coursework. Like Ian did before me.

I square my shoulders and take a quiet breath.

He was supposed to be here.

I wanted to see him here.

I wince and shove those thoughts away.

I can do this.

I clear my throat and begin. "When I was younger, I didn't give law school a second thought. I know, I know. Big surprise that as a third-grader, I didn't carry a briefcase or do my homework on yellow legal pads and call my homeroom teacher 'Your Honor.' Back then, I thought I was going to be the starting pitcher for the Dodgers."

There are a few chuckles.

"I'd have been okay with being an outfielder too. But then a strange thing happened."

A few smiles appear.

"Somehow, *shockingly*, I wasn't scouted for the majors in high school."

More laughter, and it emboldens me. Makes me think I can reach the other side of the ink on these cards.

"I figured sports broadcasting was a logical alternative. If I wasn't going to play, I could call the games.

I practiced with my phone. I'd do the play-by-play along with the radio."

A flash of memory hits me. A game we listened to five weeks ago. I did the play-by-play for Ian.

Shit.

A fist of grief grabs me, crushing my chest, throttling the major organs in my rib cage.

I need to fast forward.

"But then, I took a constitutional law class," I say, meaning to skip ahead, jump over the parts that were most likely to strangle me. I flip to the last note card and stare at the blue ink.

That's when I fell in love with law. That's when I understood why my brother had loved it, and my dad before him.

They never pushed me to pursue it. Neither one asked me to follow in their footsteps in anything but bleeding Dodger blue. But all at once, like a light turned on, I understood what I wanted in life: something bigger than me, something that made sense of the world.

The law was that. It was a set of instructions for how to live, and how to live well. That's what I needed; that's why I chose here. And that's why I'm proud to be a member of this graduating class. May we all follow the guidelines for how to live, and how to live well.

The words swirl in front of me. The letters levitate off the index cards. I'm not thinking about law at all. I'm remembering the last time I pretended to call a game as Ian lay dying.

I shut my eyes, trying to squeeze away the memory, but the dangerous images only snap into tighter focus.

I open my eyes quickly, reading the words like it's a stilted recording.

But in my head, I hear my voice, calling the game as we listened one last time.

I wonder if the hall pass extends here. Guess I'm about to find out. I shove my hands through my hair and finish, "Go Dodgers."

The dean blinks. My classmates stare. A professor furrows his brow.

I rip the index cards in half, grab my diploma from the table, and leave.

You've never seen a room go silent faster than when the guy giving the speech makes a dramatic exit two minutes in.

5

Andrew

Come to think of it, I like this hall pass.

No need to make small talk.

No need to shake hands.

Best of all, no listening to condolences.

I'm free, strutting down the street, my gangster rap blasting in my ears. No John Legend for this guy. And no tie either.

Fuck this tie.

I unknot it and toss it in a trash can.

I walk home, since it's only a couple miles away, handing my suit jacket to a homeless dude on the corner, who thanks me then asks for some chicken wings too, pointing to the convenience store on the corner. "They have a half-dozen wings for $2.99."

"Sure thing."

I pop into the store, grab some grub, and hand the man two baskets. "Here's a dozen."

He reeks of liquor and gratitude. "Thank you."

"Enjoy."

When I reach home, I change into shorts and head to the garage, Ian's dog following close behind as I park myself on the gym bench. Fitness calls.

Holland always liked my arms. Holland liked touching me. Holland liked the way I looked.

"Fuck." I can't get her out of my head, but hell if I'm working out for her.

I'm working out because I can't deal with studying for the Bar. I haven't cracked a book in weeks. I really ought to reschedule the test, but that's another thing I can't handle.

But this 150-pound weight? This, I can handle.

Exercise is what got Ian and me through the phone call no one wants to receive. Our parents were in Hawaii on a thirty-fifth-anniversary trip, doing one of those helicopter tours, when the chopper crashed.

It was quick and painless, we were told. Like that would make it easier to swallow.

Shortly after, Ian built this home gym, patted the weight bar, and declared, *"Anytime we get depressed, we lift. When we get sad, we run."*

I'd laughed. *"Dude, we are going to be so fucking fit."*

He lifted the hell out of that bench press for months. I did the same. We worked out, we ran, we talked, and we trash-talked, and somehow, we made it through.

It was only us, since our sister was long gone from our lives. She'd become a film producer, married an Indian man in the business, and moved to Mumbai with him to work in the burgeoning Bollywood industry. She'd send us cards and gifts on holidays. She'd check in with us from time to time, but it was hard to stay close when her life was so far away. It still is—though she's become a champ at weekly emails, so I have to give her credit for that.

But we didn't need Laini then. We were brothers-in-arms, and we found our way through.

We had freedom of choice. No debt, no school loans—our parents were well off, and everything that was theirs became ours. We went to the same college then the same law school. I'd join the family firm too, when I finished my studies.

The firm I now own, since it was his, and what's his is mine.

I curse as I lift the barbell.

I fucking hate owning all his shit.

I fucking hate needing to deal with all that stuff: with the firm, with the damn baseball cards, with the mutual funds, his red sports car, and the apartment in Tokyo our parents had owned. Ian spent a lot of time there during the last year, when he was in remission, seeing a doctor occasionally and seeing a woman too—Kana, the caretaker for the apartment and my brother's girlfriend.

He met her a year ago and asked her out that same night. He always said she was worth flying all those hours to spend weekends with, sometimes longer.

In the end, their relationship was short-lived, just as he'd predicted.Because his was a short-lived life, and now it's entirely up to me to decide what to do with the apartment in the Shibuya district of the neon city.

Do I keep it? Sell it? Rent it?

Selling would be easy—the place is smack dab in a trendy part of the metropolis. But renting could net a hefty monthly windfall too.

I switch to the dumbbells, working on triceps, then biceps, thinking of the empty apartment. Maybe I should treat it like an investment, and to do that, I should evaluate it closely. God knows I have the time. Yeah, I have a job whenever I want to start, but no one *needs* me to run the corporate law firm. I simply own it. The other lawyers there are aces at making that place go, go, go every day.

Maybe I should jet over to Tokyo for the summer.

I love that city, but I hate that city too. I can't think of Tokyo without Holland reappearing in my thoughts. It's what wrenched us apart three years ago when she went to nursing school there.

I finish my reps and head inside, Sandy at my

heels. I grab my phone, click on the folder with Holland's pictures in it, and open a shot of her.

It's a selfie—she's in Shibuya Crossing, the famous intersection where six roads collide. A gigantic Chihuahua stands on his hind legs on the billboard behind her, and night has fallen. The text message with it said: *I'm here, and I should be happy, but I miss you so much.*

I run my thumb over the picture. The three months we were together were so much more than a summer fling. We'd toyed with the possibility of doing a long-distance relationship, but we both had school—years of it. In the end, we'd faced the hard truth and decided that it was best to focus on studies and maybe, if fates aligned, see each other again someday.

No promises, but no doors closed either.

I thought—foolishly—that somehow everything would work out.

But distance has a way of smothering love.

Now, there's hardly any distance between us. She's mere miles away, and maybe that's why it's easier to text her.

Andrew: The reception was great. My speech lasted all of two minutes.

Holland: Was it supposed to be that short?

Andrew: I think the goal was ten or fifteen. I cut to the chase and then walked out. It was a true mic drop moment. But at least my hair looked good.

Holland: Your hair looked great. Sorry the reception sucked. I'm with London, making lasagna. Want to join us?

My shoulders tighten, and I stare at the last message like it's mocking me. Holland's hanging with her sister. Her sister is cool, and they love each other like crazy.

No fucking way can I be near that.

Shame, because her lasagna is epic.

Andrew: Nah, I need to mow the lawn. But thanks.

The lawn looks perfect, courtesy of Mrs. Callahan, and Holland knows it because she was here hours ago.

Instead of seeing them, I take half a Vicodin and watch a documentary on baboons, but I can't stop thinking of Tokyo.

6

Holland

I don't remember a time when I didn't know Andrew.

Our parents were friends, thanks to the Japan connection. When Andrew was younger, his folks were expats in Tokyo, helping run an American company overseas. Mine were in the military, but they'd bonded as Americans working in a foreign country and having roots in Southern California.

When we were both kids, our parents relocated back to the States. My family lived in San Diego, and his settled here in Los Angeles. Growing up, I saw Andrew a few times a year at family get-togethers.

I'd have been a liar if I'd said I wasn't attracted to him. I might have dreamed about him when I was in high school. I definitely fantasized about him when I was in college.

Time and distance were never on our side though—until the summer we both graduated from college. I had an internship in Los Angeles. For one perfect season, we were in the same place at the same time, and the funny thing is it all started with a possum.

I found the creature under the couch at my apartment. The first thing I did was call Andrew, since he lived so close and I don't do rodents. He told me to grab a broom, then he said, *"Screw it, I'm coming over."* A few minutes later, he swept that possum right out of the house and into the backyard. I slammed the doors shut then insisted on cooking him dinner.

Over pasta primavera we reminisced, chatting about barbecues our parents had hosted and when we'd hang out by ourselves playing video games or watching movies.

Then we moved to the sofa as we strolled down memory lane, all that talking like a slow dance bringing us closer together.

"Or how about all the times they'd send us to the store for something?" I'd asked. "And once we slipped away to a coffee shop?"

He inched closer to me, and I stared at his arms —I was such a sucker for strong arms, for *his* arms. "Those were the best lattes I'd ever had," he said, his voice a little husky.

I moved closer too, going quieter. "What about the time I found a possum in the house?"

He'd stared at me. "Tonight?"

My heart skated circles in my chest. "Yes, tonight."

Every breath was magic in the night air because I knew every breath would bring me closer to him.

"Did you plant a possum under your couch, Holland?"

"No. But I'm glad it was here."

He lifted his hand, fingering a strand of my hair. This was going to happen. This was real. "Are you glad I'm here?"

"Yes." My arms were around his neck, and my lips were on his, and all those years of attraction combusted.

His lips were soft, his jaw was stubbled, and his body was hard. Kissing him on my couch was better than I'd ever imagined. Worlds, moons, suns, and stars better, and there were so many times I'd imagined it.

With his perfect body pressed against mine, my mind was soaring and my whole body was humming.

It was the best summer of my life.

Leaving him was the hardest thing I'd ever done, but my parents made it clear—I'd earned a scholarship for nursing school in Tokyo on account of us having lived there and me speaking the language.

Anyplace else I went wouldn't be covered. Plus, they'd relocated back to Japan, choosing to retire in Kyoto. They loved the expat community and the culture, and I wanted to be near them.

I also wanted to be a nurse more than anything, so I moved around the globe, and I said goodbye to the first guy I'd ever loved.

The only guy I've ever loved.

We're finally in the same county, and if I'm only here for a little while, I don't want to waste any time. He might have turned down my lasagna invite, but I'm determined to see him again. He's the person I've always liked spending my days with, and even though I don't know where I'm going—if I'll land a job in Los Angeles or San Francisco, Seattle or Japan again—I don't want to miss a chance to see him.

I don't have a grand plan for us to get back together—I'd just rather be with him than without him right now. When I'm at the Promenade to pick up the new Kristin Hannah book, I contemplate inviting him to see a movie or grab a bite to eat, when I spot a pair of robots arguing.

Well, a guy painted in silver who does robot moves is arguing with a guy covered in gold.

"This is my turf," the silvery one spits out.

With avid eyes, I watch, then I grab my phone and hit the record button.

"Yeah? Where's the sign that says it belongs to you?"

"Everyone knows you don't infringe on another robot's territory."

The gold guy parks his hands on his hips. "Make. Me. Move."

Whoa.

Maybe it's time for me to hightail it back into the bookstore. But before I turn around, a cop breaks up the almost fight.

Cop. Possum. Robots.

I'm not saying they're connected. But Andrew would seriously get a kick out of a turf war on the Santa Monica Promenade.

I call him.

He answers immediately with a *hey*.

"Did you ever study property rights or squatter's rights or whatever you call that in law school?"

He laughs. "Yes, I did."

"I think your services might be needed, then, at the Promenade. That is, if you can handle robots for clients. The silver robot dude was really pissed at the gold one."

"Was the gold one pushing all his buttons?"

I laugh, and so does he.

"I have video. Seriously, the police were called, but no street performers were harmed." I pause, not wanting this conversation to end. No time like the present. "Hey, since you turned down my lasagna invitation, I won't take no for an answer to having lunch with me. That awesome sandwich shop that slathers everything in sriracha is calling our names."

"Is that so?"

"Yeah, can't you hear it?" I turn my voice echo-y. *"Andrew, come have a sriracha-covered turkey panini with Holland."*

More laughter comes my way. "I'll be there in thirty."

As I head to the sandwich shop, I say a silent thank you to the robots, like I did to the possum years ago.

7

Andrew

I find Holland at an outdoor table, big brown sunglasses pushed up on her head. The sun is bright, but she's not shielding her eyes. She wears a green skirt I swear she wore when we went to the movies three years ago and barely watched a scene on the screen.

My hands have been up that skirt. My fingers know the fabric and how it feels against her skin. They itch to get reacquainted.

I can smell lemon-sugar lotion on her too. Her scent will be my downfall. My blood heats as I sit next to her.

"Don't mind me. I'm baking," she says, and tilts her face to the sun. She closes her eyes and soaks in the rays, and I have free rein to look at her—at her neck, her throat, her shoulders, since she's only wearing a tank top. I want to watch her, lick her, kiss her.

She opens her eyes, sees me staring. But she doesn't look away, and neither do I.

"Have you reached the fully-cooked stage yet?"

She shakes her head. "A few more rays of sunshine are necessary for me to achieve that state of nirvana."

"It's either sunshine or sriracha that'll get you there," I say, since those are two of her favorite things.

She wiggles her eyebrows. "You know it." She dips her hand into her purse. "May I present exhibit A?"

She clicks on a video, and I catch the tail end of the robot fisticuffs. "That is excellent. And for the record, the gold one already contacted me. I'm considering taking his case."

She pumps a fist. "I knew I could find clients for you by wandering around here and observing local altercations."

The waiter arrives. She orders a sandwich, and I do the same. Same orders, same choices, same food we used to pick when we came here before.

So much is the same, and so much never will be.

Except this.

The way we talk.

The easy slide back into banter, about robots and sunshine and sandwich toppings.

When the waiter leaves, Holland makes a *ding* like a timer.

"Fully cooked now?"

She stares at her arms as if assessing them. "It appears that I am. Also, in case you were wondering, I'm still allergic to cold."

"And fog," I add, because I know this riff.

"And wind chill. The worst. Seriously. Who thought wind chill was a good idea?"

"The same person who thought icicles made sense."

"That's why I'm soaking up all this sunshine while I'm here."

"Did you find a new job yet? Are you going back to Japan?"

She holds up crossed fingers. "A few things are looking good. One in particular, but it doesn't start for another month."

One month.

The part of my brain still capable of logic knows it'll be for the best if I leave for Tokyo stat and figure shit out without her *there*, without me *here*. She smells so fucking good that I want to abandon everything and spend the summer bantering and watching her sunbathe.

But it's hard to plan with her around.

It's hard to think straight when she's the only

thing I'm certain I want. When I'm positive her touch would erase the pain.

Her bare legs are close enough I could run a hand over her knee, watch her shiver and smile. She'd ask me to do it again. My palms ache to touch her, like her skin is a magic potion, a pill to make me happy again. I'm filled with complete emptiness and complete longing at the same time, only there's not enough space in me for both.

Longing wins. Longing always wins with her.

She's the last time I was truly happy, and I want that again so badly I'll do nearly anything to get it, like spending time with her in this

"just friends" state that I don't understand. But I'm powerless to resist it.

8

Holland

We wander along the Promenade, popping into gift shops and checking out random items like candlestick holders and jewelry racks that are as big as bureaus. We dart into a soap store and sniff spruce- and grapefruit-scented ones, giving them a thumbs-up, then turning up our noses collectively at one that smells like leather. When we reach the end of the Promenade, I gesture to the cinema down the block, grasping for one more chance to spend time with him. One more moment that won't be too raw, too risky.

"Do you want to go to the movies?"

"The movies?"

"Yeah, that thing where they project famous

actors in impossible situations on the screen?"

In a perfect deadpan, he answers, "I'm familiar with the concept."

"The more stuff that blows up, the better," I add.

"No Oscar contenders, no quiet dramas, no period romances with English accents."

"No way. We want fires, and we want chase scenes, and we want dudes jumping out of tenth-story windows and then running through the streets like it didn't even hurt."

Life is full of enough family drama. We don't need it on the screen.

We. We. We.

Here I am, acting like we're a *we* again, going through the same motions, playing our parts.

It hardly feels like playing.

"There's a new Jason Statham flick at the theater down the block, I hear," I say, flashing back to the last time we were there three years ago.

We didn't watch the film at all.

My cheeks flame.

We were animals. We were practitioners of PDA. His hands were up my skirt—the same skirt I'm wearing now—and he made me see stars as a building on screen blew up.

Heat flares through me.

I wave a hand in front of my face before I go up in flames. Spending time with him is dangerous. I like him too much, I want him too much. The trouble is his grief is too new, too raw. I don't want to be his crutch, and I can tell I am.

"I forgot. I have an appointment. Another time."

"Another time?" he asks, like those two words are alien.

I turn away so he can't see my face. "Yes, I have somewhere to be."

He says my name more urgently. "Holland."

I turn around, and he's a snapshot of a man caught taking a step toward a woman.

I'm a woman wanting to catch him. That's what the camera captures when it trains on me. "What is it?"

"I've been thinking of what to do this summer."

"What do you want to do?" I ask tightly, possibilities winding up in me, wishes and hopes I can't let myself entertain.

His phone buzzes. He grabs it from his pocket and swipes the screen. "It's Jeremy. I told him I'd meet him for a beer. We'll talk later?"

I nod. "Of course. Absolutely. You should go."

"I should go."

I try not to let on how much I don't want him to leave as I say goodbye and wrap my arms around him in a hug that lasts longer than it should.

Then it lasts a few more seconds still as his arms tighten around me, and I lean my face into his neck, stealing a quick inhale of his scent. He's the scent I like best.

Moments later, I untangle myself from him and watch him walk away, even though I ache seeing him go.

Sometimes, I think we're both stuck in the same quicksand of the past and the present. The only way to escape is to stop letting my head get in the way of my heart.

9

Andrew

The next day I check the mail for the first time in days. There are no more sympathy cards. They have all come and gone. The *sorry*s, the prayers, the *my thoughts are with you*s are over. Everyone has said what they need to say, and everyone has moved on to their noisy, everyday lives. They're all back on the merry-go-round of life—a merry-go-round I'm nowhere near ready to climb onto.

The mail brings only memories. A cooking magazine. A baseball card catalog. Ian's alumni journal.

I drop the catalogs and everything else from the mailbox into the green recycling bin at the end of the driveway. As the papers fall, I spot something that doesn't look like a catalog. It's a letter, addressed to me, my name written in calligraphy with some sort of felt-tip pen. The postmark is Japanese, and the name in the return address—*Kana Miyoshi*—startles me.

Holland's friend.

The caretaker for the apartment.

My brother's girlfriend.

I walk back into my eerily quiet house and sit at the kitchen counter. My hand shakes as I slide a thumb under the envelope flap. My heart is beating quickly too, like I expect this letter to unleash secrets.

I turn to the dog, who's stretched out on the nearby couch. Her legs poke up in the air, the back ones looking like drumsticks with those meaty thighs she has.

"What do you think it says, Sandy?"

She tilts her head toward me and waits for an answer.

I pull out the letter, and as I unfold it, I'm not in Los Angeles anymore, but thousands of miles away. I can see and smell and hear and taste Tokyo. Even the paper looks Asian.

Dear Andrew—

Hey! I tried to email you, but I never heard back. Perhaps it went to spam? I thought I had your phone number, but I might be a digit off since I kept reaching a dry cleaner in

*Santa Monica. I can tell you there are very many afford-
able options for suits there!*

*In any case, I'm resorting to this most old-fashioned
method of communication. As you may know, I'm the
caretaker for your apartment on Maruyamacho Street,
and I was also a good friend of Ian's.*

I smile at the euphemism.

*We were cleaning the apartment recently, and we discov-
ered several medication prescriptions on the shelves.*

She lists the medicines and notes whether each
bottle had been opened. Most are marked as
unopened. Odd.

*Would you like us to make arrangements to ship them to
you, leave them here, or dispose of them? I'm sorry to
trouble you with this seemingly trivial matter, but we try
to be careful with how we handle medication and other
related items. Please advise.*

Also, since I am writing to you in a professional capacity, as well as a personal one, it is customary in situations like this for us to inform the family of the personal effects in the apartment.

She lists things like clothes and photos and other items, but what catches my attention are the next few lines.

There are also several crossword puzzle books, a stub from a John Legend concert, some cards and your brother's favorite Dodgers cap. Perhaps you know it? It is the one that says World Series Champions, even though they didn't win. He had a friend in charge of the printing of the caps so they would be ready for either team—he snagged one before the boxes were sent to a village in Africa. He must have left it here on his last visit in late February. He wore it when we visited his favorite temple. I have a photo from that day, which I can send, along with any other items you might want.

He was an amazing man, the most joyful at times, and very funny too. He liked to take me to tea with him occasionally at the Tatsuma Teahouse, and he said playfully he was simply following doctor's orders by going there. While we were together, he told me such wonderful stories of life back home and stories of you. I am sorry we never met, and please accept my deep regrets, once again, that I couldn't attend the service. Ian expressly asked that I not attend, and I protested many times. But, as he often did, he had the last word. Please know Ian was so proud of you, and of how hard you worked, especially during the last year of school. He talked about you all the time, always with so much happiness in his eyes. He loved you so.

Best,
Kana

There's a phone number and an email address.

I jam the heel of my hand against my eye and swallow roughly, viciously, trying to edge past the aggressive lump in my throat. I stare at the dog until my vision clears again.

I set down the letter and step away from the counter. Breathing out hard, I pace through the living room to the sliding glass door. I shove it open and inhale the thick June air. I cut a path across the yard, around the pool, vaguely aware the dog is trotting behind me.

I turn to her.

"Why didn't I go with him?" I huff in frustration.

"I should have gone with him on one of his trips in the last year."

Sandy stares, head tilted, wagging her tail.

But there was no reason for me to go to Tokyo. He was in remission, and he was busy with Kana there. I was buried in coursework, an internship, and studying for the Bar. The final year of law school leaves no breathing room for any extracurricular activities.

I want to smack myself for not going with him at least once, for not getting to know the one doctor he briefly saw there.

He told me to stay behind—to focus on school and the Bar. *That's all that matters to me. Finish your JD, don't take care of your big brother.*

I drag a hand through my hair and curse. "I fucking wanted to take care of you, asshole."

But now I wonder what those trips meant to him, and the role the doctor he saw—Takahashi or something—played in his life.

I scratch my head, trying to make sense of the teahouse and the temple. Ian e-mailed me when he traveled to Tokyo, told me he was doing well, singing karaoke with Kana and eating fish at the market with her too, but he never mentioned a temple. He definitely never said a word about Tatsuma anything, and certainly not whether a good doctor had sent him to a teahouse, of all places.

I'm not religious, and I'm not spiritual. I don't

know if I believe in anything, yet here is this letter arriving just days after I've started thinking about the apartment in Tokyo, and it feels like a message from *out there*.

This is what I'm supposed to be doing before I buckle down and focus on work. Figuring out how Ian was the *most joyful* when he was dying. Because I'm living, and I sure as hell don't feel anything but empty.

I flip open my laptop and plug *Tatsuma Teahouse* into the browser, but I can't find a website for it, only a location in Shibuya on a few city guides. There's a short review on one of the sites, so I copy the Japanese words into an online translator and read the results.

"Tatsuma Tea is a very healing cure."

Is this a result of a bad translation? Or did he turn to some other kind of cure, and that's why some of his meds were left unopened? Did he go overseas searching for a brass ring that didn't exist?

I grab my phone and call Holland. I skip the hello and launch into questions. "Did Ian stop taking his meds when he was in Tokyo?"

She makes a startled noise. "What?"

"Do you know if he stopped taking his meds when he was there? You saw him."

"I didn't see him that much," she says gently. "And I don't think so, but he was in remission most of the time."

"He still had meds for remission," I say, since Ian was on those meds for a while, well before he first noticed signs in January that the cancer might be recurring. The disease roared all the way back in March, two months before it KO'd him.

"I'm aware of that."

"Did he stop taking them *here*?"

"There were things your cousin Kate and I cleaned out after . . ." She lets her voice go. Finds it again. "But I didn't inventory his meds. I didn't count pills. Besides, there weren't many left when . . ." Another abandoned sentence. Another side effect of death. Words go AWOL. "So we just got rid of what was left." She clears her throat. "What's going on?"

I swallow hard. "There are things I need to understand."

"What? What do you need to understand?" Her voice wavers, and something in it—maybe the threat of her tears—stabs at me.

I want to tell Holland. I want to show her the note so we can devise a plan together, a map of what's next. My decision to go to Tokyo is the first thing that's felt like a spark, like a flash of light and color, in months. Because it's *something*, it's movement, it's not just the vast expanse of endless, hollow days.

But I remember the whiplash of lunch the other day.

Of every day with us.

The *you're beautiful*.

The *it's okay.*

The *let's see a movie.*

The *I have an appointment.*

We are both attracting and repelling each other, and right now I need facts, not endless feelings for the girl I want to fuck and kiss and bury my sorrows in as I fuck her some more.

But I'm not fucking her or kissing her. Because she's not mine, and I can't get caught up in her again.

"I'll call you back later," I say.

"Promise," she says, a flash of urgency in her tone.

"I promise."

"We can get Chinese," she adds.

"Yeah."

Hanging up, I grab my phone, keys, and wallet.

I could call or e-mail Kana, but I don't want to say the wrong thing to her.

I head to see someone else. Someone who knew my brother on this side of the world.

10

Andrew

At the hospital cafeteria, Trina shakes three sugar packets crisply between her thumb and forefinger. She rips open her sweet trifecta and dumps it into her coffee. "Fuel," she says, tapping the paper cup. She wears blue scrubs, a white lab coat, and has her long black hair looped back into a ponytail at the nape of her neck. "You want one?"

I shake my head.

She waggles the cup at me. "I'd much rather give you this than the other thing."

"I'm not here for that."

She lets out an exhale. "Good. So what's the story, morning glory?"

I tell Trina about the letter as clinically as I can,

like an unbiased reporter, because I want her unbiased report in return. I tell her about the absence of meds at my house.

"You're going to go, right?" she asks.

I don't answer right away because I expected more back-and-forth.

"You're going to go and meet this woman and read the cards, and see this temple and go to this teahouse?" She chugs half her coffee. I wonder if it burns her throat.

"You *really* think I should go there?" I figured I was crazy, casting about for something, anything, and Trina would knock sense into me. But logical, rational, sensible Trina thinks Tokyo is a good idea.

She nods several times. "Next flight. Go."

"Why?"

"First off, because of the meds. That's a little weird if he wasn't taking them, and to leave them behind. That doesn't sound like Ian. It's one thing to stop meds when you're at the end, but a few months before then? Cancer patients usually take their meds, especially when his returned so aggressively. Because, you know, meds fight the cancer."

My heart drops, sagging heavily under the weight of the possibility that my brother simply stopped wanting to fight.

That notion feels so foreign, so at odds with the man I knew, that I don't know how to fit it into the picture of him. He was a lawyer, and a damn good one, like our dad before us. Like I'm going to be. The Peterson men know how to fight. It's in our blood.

"I should go to Tokyo, find Takahashi, and ask if my brother was taking his medicine or not?" I ask, sounding like the parent checking up on the sick kid.

"He must have had a reason for not taking them. Do you want to know?"

Desperately. "What about the whole doctor-patient confidentiality thing? I thought it was against the rules or something."

She shrugs. "Technically. But that's all about getting sued, and this isn't a TV crime drama. There isn't a trial going on where someone's being compelled to testify. Plus, in some countries, the doctors are accustomed to talking to the family. Friends of mine who've worked in Asia have said as much. The family sometimes learns stuff before the patient does."

"But what do you think this temple and teahouse is all about? Is that like some new medical treatment for cancer? Some alternative healing or whatever?" I shrug in question. "That doesn't sound like Ian. Not at all. He was very traditional. No voodoo shit, he'd say."

Trina doesn't answer right away. She takes another drink. "I don't have the answers, Andrew. But whatever it was, it sounds like a good thing, like spending his last few months in that manner was a good way to go." Her voice softens as if she's talking to a worried patient. She reaches a hand out and places it on mine. "Drinking tea. Sharing stories. That sounds nice, doesn't it?"

I nod briefly and look away. I'm glad he wasn't in pain every single second. I hate that my strong, tough brother, the man who taught me how to tie a tie, how to fix a flat tire, how to ask a girl on a date was even in pain at all. Watching him throw up, watching him wither away after his treatments—nothing prepared me for that. Not even losing our parents first. Because when they went, it was a quick, clean slash of lightning. With Ian, it was a relentless downpour.

For years.

"Hey," she says softly. "Do you need anything before you go?"

I wiggle my eyebrows. "A couple more?"

She looks around the cafeteria and shakes her head. "Shh."

"Just kidding." *I'm not kidding at all.*

She walks me out to my car and gives me a hug in the parking lot. "I'm here if you need anything. If you have questions, text me."

"I will, Trina."

She takes a breath. "I found a picture. Of the three of us. That night we were all up late studying, and you convinced Ian we needed to go to the pier and ride the roller-coaster."

"He was always a sucker for the roller-coaster."

She reaches into the pocket of her white coat and takes out an envelope. "I had a copy printed."

She hands me the envelope and says goodbye. When I get in the car, I slide my finger along the seal, opening it. Ian's leaning against the pier, looking casual, Trina's smiling, and I'm right next to them, laughing at who knows what. I don't look like the kid brother who tagged along. Ian never made me feel like I was four years younger, or like I was an obligation.

I miss him every damn day.

I set the photo on my dashboard and ball up the envelope. Something stops me midway through. I uncrinkle it and fish around inside. In the corner of the envelope is Trina's parting gift.

It won't get me far, but I won't complain about a few more goodies. I peer around to see if she's still in the parking lot, but she's gone. She's sticking her neck out for me.

I send a quick text to say thank you, stuff the pills in my wallet, and take off.

I have a trip to plan, a treasure map to follow.

There's only one thing left to take care of.

11

Andrew

Two hours later, Holland's at my door, holding cartons of Chinese food, her black canvas purse on her shoulder. "I don't think the rice is sizzling anymore, but the pepper steak will taste good if we heat it up. Can I come in?"

"Anytime."

Truer words . . .

She walks straight to my kitchen and takes out two ceramic bowls, pours the soup into one, and pops it into the microwave. She knows my house. It's scary sometimes, how much she knows about me. She knows what foods I like, what books I read, what movies I'll watch all the way through and which ones I've walked out on. I know little details about her too

—she's a card shark and wins at nearly every card game I've ever played with her, she likes simple clothes and simple styles, and she'd happily serve this dinner on her own, but she'll be even happier if I help her.

I root around in the utensil drawer for spoons then grab plates. We quickly work together to heat and serve then sit down at the counter, a plate of Chinese food for each of us.

Like we used to do. There's so much familiarity, and I don't know how to separate the way I used to feel for her from the way I want her now. But those feelings—the past and the present ones—are a knot inside my chest I can't untwist.

Getting away from here might help.

"I know how much you like Captain Wong's," she says.

"I do. But that name kills me every time. Why the hell is it *Captain*? Is he flying a ship full of Chinese food?" I affect a sci-fi voice. "Hello. I am Captain Wong."

"I have come to take over your planet," she adds. I laugh, and she does too, and then her laughter fades. We eat in silence for a minute.

"So are you going to Tokyo?" she asks.

I set down the spoon. "How did you figure it out?"

Her blue eyes pierce me. "I know you."

The way she looks at me—my heart pounds

against my skin, trying to make a mutinous escape to land in her hands.

"Yeah? What do you know?"

Does she know how much I want her? How much I never forgot us? How much I wanted to grab her all those nights she was at my house last month, press her to the wall, and kiss her till I forgot the world around me?

She has to know. I'm so transparent.

"You won't rest till you understand." A flicker of worry is in her tone.

"Is that so?"

"That is so." Her eyes linger on me, soft and full of kindness.

Earlier, I didn't want to show her the note, but that's the part of me that's prone to shutting down. I don't have to with her. Hell, she didn't even judge me for hitting the car. I'd rather let her in than keep her out.

"I need you to see this letter. I need to know what you think of it. Help me read between the lines." I reach for the letter at the edge of the counter where I left it, and slide it to her. "What can you tell me about any of this? You know Kana—she's your friend."

She reads it, swiping at her cheek at one point, erasing a rebel tear. When she finishes, she looks up. "I didn't go with him to the teahouse and the temple. I only saw him a few times when he was in Tokyo. He wasn't there to see me—he was there to see her."

"Do you think I'm grasping at straws? I read this, and I feel like I don't know him."

"It might feel that way now, but you knew him better than anyone."

That's what I want, and yet, this new wrinkle eludes me. Not the what, but the *why*. The trouble is I only possess the answer at the end of the equation —it looks like he stopped taking the meds. The law school part of me knows there are three options based on that evidence: either he ceased taking the meds in lieu of an alternative, or he wanted to get life over with, or he stopped for some other reason.

Whichever it is, I don't know the *why*, and I need to know.

The need bangs insistently on the back of my brain, like a drip of the faucet that won't turn off.

I take a deep breath and voice my hope. "I want to believe I knew him well."

She tilts her head, studying my face. "But you don't believe that?"

I don't answer her directly. I'm not sure I'm ready to admit that fear—that I didn't know him as well as I hope. "Is there some reason I shouldn't go?" I ask, because the one reason I'd stay is if she asked me to.

She pushes her plate away. "You should go."

Her command both emboldens me and crushes me.

Tell me you miss me. Tell me to spend the summer with you.

She inches her hand across the counter just a little bit closer, and that hand, I want to grab it and hold on. I glance at our fingers, so close all it would take is one of us giving an inch.

Give. Take. Come. Stay.

I can feel the warmth from her hand. One stretch for us to reconnect, so I wait. Wait for her to put her hands on my face and press her lips against mine and kiss me like it's been killing her not to.

But I can't wait.

I break first, saying her name in a lonely, desperate rasp. "Holland."

"Andrew." Her voice is a whisper.

"Go with me," I blurt out.

She blinks. "What?"

I shake my head.

Leaving the kitchen, I stalk to the living room, pacing like I can sort out what to do if I get just a few feet away from her.

She's right behind me, her hand on my arm. "Say it again."

I swivel around, and with her blue eyes on mine, her body close, I break to pieces. With her, my heart beats too fast, my blood pumps too quickly. I have no will to tell her to stop being so near to me but not near enough to make everything better.

"Say what again?" I ask, as if I've forgotten.

"Ask me," she presses.

And she wins. She fucking wins. "Go with me. Come with me."

She squeezes my arm. "Is that what you want?'

I cup her cheeks. She gasps. I've shocked her. Let's shock her some more.

Her lips part, and she whispers my name. "Andrew."

It's like the stars are glowing. Like the sky is blazing at night. "You know what I want."

"Sometimes I feel like I don't know you anymore."

"But you do," I insist.

"Do I?"

I bend closer, giving her the time, the space, anything she needs to stop me. She doesn't. She lifts her chin, an invitation.

I RSVP.

I drop my mouth to hers, and the second we make contact, I'm high.

She tastes fantastic—like strawberries and desire. I brush my lips over hers, and this is like riding a bike. I will never forget how she likes to be kissed. How she craves a slow build. How she wants to get lost in kisses that start as whispers.

Her lips dust mine, and a sweet sigh falls from her mouth. I catch it on my lips and swallow it, and her lips part wider. She opens for me, and I kiss her a little harder, a little rougher, until she's angling her body to mine, and we connect.

This is the way we were.

We can be that way again.

She can be the one to make me happy.

I lift her up, and she wraps her legs around my waist as I carry her to the couch.

As I lower her, our mouths disengage, and I wait for a sign. A cue. A word like *stop*. But it doesn't come. Instead, she slides a hand into my hair and yanks my face down to hers.

"Kiss me again," she commands.

I smile as I kiss her lips, as I travel over her jaw, as I nibble on her ear.

She arches against me and lets out a moan.

This kiss isn't a solo rider. It's heading to all the lands where we used to travel. Since she returned, the energy between us has pulsed. The air we breathe has been charged.

She wraps her legs around me, gripping me tight, tugging me close. She seals her mouth to mine, a hungry, consuming creature. *Yes, Holland, you can have me.*

When she kisses me, my world spins on its axis. When she ropes her hands in my hair and pulls me closer, I'm home. She's better than any pill. She's stronger than any combination of chemicals. The effect she has on my brain is only bested by how she exhilarates my heart. It ricochets in my chest as I kiss her, as I rock into her, as I can't get close enough to her.

She writhes and pushes and presses, and it's all I've ever wanted. It's all I need to get through a day.

She lets out a little cry chased by a long, lingering one. She's not stopping either. She wants this. She wants me to grind against her till she gets there.

God, there's nothing I want more in the universe than to get her off.

My entire body sizzles. My brain goes haywire, all hot static and mind-bending pleasure.

Endorphins explode in me. I feel something good, something great, something mind-blowing.

I want to spend the summer fucking her. Making her come over and over. Making her fall apart. I want to numb my head with pleasure, cover my broken heart with sex.

Sex is the answer. Sex with her will make every second better.

She seems to have the same idea, but then her hands slam on my chest, and she pushes me.

I rise, breathing hard, breathing recklessly. "Are you okay?"

She nods, panting. "I want to, but we can't."

"Why?"

"Andrew," she says, like I should know.

"Why?" I ask again.

She shakes her head, doesn't answer me.

"Are you sorry we kissed?"

"No." She straightens her shirt and sits up. "But there's something you need to know."

Nothing good has ever come of those words. My shoulders slump. "What do I need to know?"

"I was already planning to go back. To Tokyo."

I don't process the enormity of her statement. Only the immediacy of it. "You were?"

She nods. "The job I mentioned? The one that was looking promising?"

"Yeah?"

"I got it, and it's in Tokyo." A sneaky smile spreads on her face.

I'm not clear on how to read her. "Is that a secret or something?"

"No. I wasn't sure how to tell you I might be returning."

"Why?" I raise an eyebrow.

She shakes her head but doesn't answer me directly. "The job sounds great. One of my former coworkers referred me to another medical center. They have some new shifts opening. They want nurses who speak English and Japanese."

"Sounds like exactly what you do," I say slowly, because there's not much blood rushing to my brain to help make sense of her words.

"Andrew," she says, demanding my attention, "the reason I said I wasn't sure how to tell you is . . . because I'd have missed you."

My heart squeezes. "I'd have missed you."

"And I didn't want to face saying goodbye to you again."

My heart lurches toward her. *Don't say goodbye*, I want to tell her. Instead, I say in a dry husk of a voice, "Saying goodbye is hard."

I can't say another fucking goodbye.

"But maybe we don't have to yet," she says with a hopeful smile. "Since I'm going back there, and you're going, I want to go with you. Help you when you need it. I don't start my job for a few more weeks, so I can be"—she pauses, quirks up her lips—"your sidekick. Will you let me?"

For a moment—no, for several long moments— I'm not sure I heard her right. I suspect I'm hopped up on too many pills, but I count back through the day, and I haven't had any.

Is she really saying this? Truly meaning this?

Her and me? Figuring shit out?

We didn't do that before.

This is a brand-new agenda. A temporary one, but at least it's something.

For now.

Those two conditional words reverberate.

This is *for now.*

But *for now* is all I have.

Besides, when I look back on my life, am I going to regret not going surfing, not taking a trip to Italy, or not saying yes to having Holland by my side as I try to understand the person I loved most?

Like I could say no to her.

"Yes."

* * *

We don't make out again. Instead, we make plans, booking flights and emailing Kana. I let her know I'm heading to Tokyo and would love to see her. As we go into full-on practical trip mode, we turn on a movie in the background. As the hero races a motorcycle down the steps of a historical building, Holland falls asleep on my couch.

It's not cold, but I cover her with a blanket. I watch her doze for a minute, a strand of her long hair falling over her mouth. Her lips flutter, trying to blow the hair away. I adjust her hair for her, tucking the strand behind her ear.

My lips form words, quiet, nearly silent words.

I love you so much it hurts, and it hurts so good. Keep making it hurt. I need it. I need you.

When I get into my bed, I'm keenly aware of her in my house, as if I can somehow hear the rise and fall of her breathing, the flutter of her sleeping eyelids, from a floor above. I imagine her waking, walking up the stairs, heading down the hall, and standing in my doorway, a sliver of moonlight through the window sketching her in the dark. I would speak first, telling her the truth—that I'm still completely in love with her. That nothing has changed for me.

Everything else is frayed around the edges. This —how I feel for Holland—is the only thing in my life that has remained the same. Everyone I have loved is gone. Except her. Holland is the before and the after.

She'd say the words back to me, that she feels the same. Like she's found the thing she's been looking for.

Come find me, come find me, come find me.

* * *

In the morning, I find her in my kitchen making toast.

"I am the world's deepest sleeper," she announces by way of a greeting. "I didn't wake up once."

"Sometimes you need to sleep through the night."

"I might be in love with your couch."

I look away as I sit at the counter on one of the stools. The toast pops up, and she begins to spread butter on it.

"Are we doing this?" I ask.

"Going to Tokyo together?"

"Yes." I clench my fists, waiting for her to tell me it was all a fevered dream.

She nods, and I exhale all the breaths in the county. "We are, but there's one thing I need you to know."

I groan. "Stop saying stuff like that."

She puts her hand on my arm. One touch, and I'm lit up. "The reason I stopped you last night?"

"Right when it was getting good?" I ask, lifting a brow.

She smiles, a flirty little grin that threatens to destroy me. "It messes with my head too much."

"It messes with mine in a good way."

"I mean it," she presses.

"How does it mess with your head?"

She takes my hand, threads her fingers through mine. "It makes me think we can go back to how we were. But I can't take advantage of you right now."

"Please," I scoff, "take advantage of me. I should be so lucky."

"You're grieving. It would be wrong."

"I don't mind that kind of wrong. I can handle all kinds of wrong." Apparently, I haven't lost the ability to flirt with her.

She squeezes my fingers. She's doing a terrible job of not taking advantage of me. I loop mine tighter around hers. Even holding her hand turns me on.

She meets my eyes. "I know, but it's going to do a number on me."

"Is it against the nurses' code?"

With her free hand, she taps her chest. "It's against *my* code."

"You weren't against it last night." Damn, I am going to be one fine attorney after all, especially when it involves negotiating the prospect of nudity.

"It's hard for me to think straight when you touch me," she whispers.

This doesn't make anything easier. She's making everything harder. "Are you asking me to be the strong one?"

A guilty little smile is her answer. "Maybe I am."

"You're fighting a losing battle, but I'll do my best. But let me give you a tip."

She arches a brow in question.

"Maybe if you want me to be the strong one, you ought to let go of my hand."

She drops her hold on me. "I didn't realize I was holding your hand. It feels so normal. That's the thing. That's the challenge."

Touching me is her normal.

I'm not strong enough to be the strong one, but I'm greedy enough to pretend that I will be, and it feels good.

For the first time in weeks, I feel . . . lighter.

"Let's get out of town."

12

Holland

I roll my clothes, lining up the fabric in little tubes.

London grabs a red shirt, scrunching it even tighter. "You can fit even more."

"I know," I say, working my packing magic with my sister. "But I don't want to exceed the weight limit."

With her light-blue eyes, she scans my bag. "I'm betting it's under fifty pounds by a hair."

"Only one way to find out."

My little sister—two years younger than my twenty-five—scurries out of the bedroom and snags the scale from the bathroom. Setting it down on the floor, she hauls the suitcase on it.

She thrusts her arms in the air in victory. "Forty-nine-point-nine." Shimmying her hips, she sings, "I've still got it."

"I hope you have it for a long, long time."

London is a flight attendant, based here but traveling to Asia often, so my parents and I see her a lot. Packing is in her blood. She's said to me before, *"I've never met a suitcase I couldn't pack better."*

London looks at her watch. "I need to take off. I have a pickup. I hardly ever get the Europe routes, but this time I'm going to Amsterdam."

"Lucky you." That's her favorite city.

She says it makes her feel closer to me when she travels there. I tease her and tell her the same about all of England. If we'd had another sibling, we joke she'd have been named Vienna, and then we'd agree how lucky we are not to have been conceived in Prague or Portugal, or Kyoto and Tokyo for that matter.

She turns around, but when she reaches the doorway, she stops and looks over her shoulder at me. "Are you really doing this?"

"I am. I have a new job. I have my apartment still in Tokyo—I rented it out on Airbnb the last month, but the renters are done, so I still have my place."

"I'm not talking about your apartment, for God's sake."

"Then what are you talking about?"

She sighs and comes back to me. "I'm talking about *him*. Be careful."

I shoot her a quizzical look. "Why do you say that?"

"Because you think you can save him."

I scoff. "I don't think that."

But I want to—to save him from all his heartache.

"You've wanted to save the entire world ever since you took care of Grandpa."

"No," I protest. "That's just when I knew I wanted to be a nurse."

"To you, it's one and the same."

I swallow hard. "But what's so wrong with that? It's who I am."

I've known since I was twelve what I wanted to do with my life. I've known since I watched my dad's father forget how to find the grocery store, what year it was, then his own son's name.

I've known it since I took care of my grandpa, making his oatmeal, reminding him who I was, playing Candy Land when everything else became too hard. Then Go Fish when Candy Land became calculus to him.

A lump rises in my throat. There hasn't been a time in my life when I didn't want to help. It's a cellular thing for me, and I can't escape from it.

London clasps my shoulder. "I don't want you thinking you can nurse your ex-boyfriend back to happy."

"I'm not trying to be his nurse."

"You were definitely playing the nurse with his brother."

I stare at her. "That's not fair. I wasn't playing anything. I *was*. I was there the last week of his life, giving him comfort care. I watched him take his last breath. Don't tell me I was playing," I say, my voice rising with my anger. "There was nothing pretend about that."

"I don't mean it like that," London grits out.

I park my hands on my hips. "Then how do you mean it?"

"You're so willing to drop everything when someone wants help." She places her palms together. "And that's part of what makes you a beautiful, wonderful woman. But don't lose sight of yourself."

She's wrong. I didn't lose sight of myself. I was helping a friend. "Kana asked me to come back here and look after him. Ian was very explicit in his instructions. He didn't want her to watch him die. He said he couldn't bear it, so she asked me to look after him in his final days. How was I supposed to say no to that?"

She softens. "You weren't. But look at you. You're still all tangled up in their family."

I spread my arms wide. "News flash: I've been tangled up in their family for a long time. It's been that way since I can remember. You can thank Mom and Dad for that."

She laughs. "True, that. Parents are always to blame."

"I blame them, then. I absolutely blame them for dragging us up to Los Angeles every time they wanted to hang out with the Petersons. It's their stupid fault I fell for him, and it's their fault I had to go to freaking Japan to get my degree."

"I'm with you. We can blame them for everything," she says with a smile. She opens her arms. "Bring it in for a hug."

I sigh heavily but step closer. "Don't think you can make it up to me so easily."

She wraps her arms around me, her silver bracelets jangling near my ears. "You never stay mad."

I huff, because she's right.

"I worry about Andrew," she says in a soft but firm tone. "He's a mess, and he probably thinks you're the one to rescue him."

I flash back to the other night, to the way he climbed over me, moved me under him. How he kissed me—like he was pouring his soul into me. I could taste his grief, salty and bitter. But it tasted like wild desire too. Like getting lost and being found. Like I wanted another serving, and then another.

Maybe I want to be needed that badly, and that's the big risk. I desperately want to heal him, but I know I have to keep those instincts at bay for my own mental health. And honestly, for his too.

"I promise I won't try to Florence Nightingale him."

London brushes a strand of my hair. "Good. He's so consuming sometimes, and you give so freely."

"I can handle it. I'm not the one going through something."

"We're all going through something."

I give her the side-eye. "Losing your rose-gold iPhone doesn't count."

"That was awful," she howls. "Especially since it had my special engraving on it. No one ever found it."

"It's gone to the great iPhone graveyard in the sky."

"I mourn it daily. Life hasn't been the same."

I shoo her to the door. "Go, or you'll be late for your pickup, and you'll lose a shoe while running through the airport, and that'll be the next terrible thing you endure."

She shudders. "I do like my shoes. That would be awful to lose one."

* * *

That afternoon I print my boarding pass for tomorrow.

Three years ago, I boarded the same flight.

Andrew took me to the airport then, and we were *those people*. The ones you walk past and think *oh please*. The long, never-ending goodbye. The final embrace that lasts too long. The last kiss—his hands holding my face. The tears streaking down. Then the staring out the little oval window for hours.

I was only twenty-two. What did I know about falling in love at twenty-two? But what does anyone ever know?

When I arrived in Tokyo, I missed him with a profound ache I didn't think I'd ever get over. Letting go of someone you love when you're still loving them is a special kind of awful, like a bruise that twinges every second of every day.

But then, the ache ebbed and the longing dimmed.

We did what we promised each other. I became absorbed in my studies and the world in which I lived, and it stopped me missing him so badly. Time worked its magic, since time is the only thing that can.

But did it?

As I fold the boarding pass and slide it into my purse, I ask myself if my sister is right—am I too tangled up in him? Or have I never truly unraveled myself?

Sure, a big part of me wants to dive headfirst back into his kisses and spending all my nights in his arms.

The problem is, in a few weeks, we'll still face the same challenge—the ocean between us.

And a whole lot more, since life is a cruel bitch, and she's upped the ante this time around by breaking my man in a whole new way.

My man.

He still feels like mine. I don't want him to be anyone else's.

But I have to be stronger than my own wishes. Loving him the way I want might not help him.

And loving him *truly* might mean letting him heal independently of a healer.

Independent of me.

13

Andrew

Ian adopted this dog two years ago, and she's named after the greatest Dodgers pitcher ever, Sandy Koufax, a lefty like Ian, and a fighter too.

"We should name her Sandy," Ian said as I drove us home from the shelter while he petted the little border collie-Lab puppy sitting in his lap.

I shook my head. "Sandy is a guy. This dog is a girl."

"No shit, Sherlock."

I rolled my eyes. "You want to name your girl dog after a guy?"

He stared at me as I drove. "Did I not teach you better than this?"

"What? What lesson did I fail to learn now?" I

asked, as if I were frustrated, but I wasn't. I liked that we were acting normal. That the cancer might be destroying cells, but it wasn't killing his funny bone, it wasn't damaging his sense of self.

He pointed a finger at me. "You're not a sexist pig."

I laughed. "I'm definitely not a sexist pig. You know that."

Ian narrowed his mostly-missing eyebrows at me and hugged the dog tightly. "Sandy is not a sexist pig. She doesn't mind being named after a man."

I cracked up as I drove. "So you naming a chick dog after a guy athlete means you're not sexist? I feel like that might be the definition of sexist."

"Watch it, or we'll start calling you Andrea."

"You and the dog are a *we* now?"

He'd nodded, grinning wickedly. "Yes. I've decided this is my one chance to be totally off my rocker and do whatever weird shit I want. Including calling the dog and me a we."

"Memo to Ian—you've been weird your whole life. It didn't start when your cells metastasized."

He liked it when I didn't shirk away from the reality—he didn't want me to whisper the name of his disease or call it *the C word. "It is what it is, and I'm going to kick cancer's motherfucking ass."*

Back then, I'd slowed at a light and reached out to stroke the dog's chin. "I like this non-sexist woman-power canine."

Sandy was a fitting name for the dog. Sandy Koufax wasn't just the greatest pitcher ever. He was resilient. He played through pain, pitching with a damaged elbow, throwing heat with injured fingers. The name would be a fitting tribute, not just to a baseball legend, but to my brother.

In the back of my mind, I knew the dog would outlive Ian. But I wanted to believe that my brother —who was kick-ass at everything he did—would drop-kick cancer's ass too.

Now Sandy is all mine. She always was mine, truth be told—even though we called her Ian's dog, she made her allegiance clear. The first night home she slept in my bed.

I'm going to miss this dog like crazy.

With Sandy waiting in the front seat of the car, I knock on Mrs. Callahan's door.

She opens it in seconds, and a smile launches across her weathered face. "Hello, Andrew. What can I do for you?"

"I'm going away for a little while. A few weeks, I think. Can you—?"

"Consider it done. The lawn will be a gleaming shade of emerald when you return, and the flowers will be blooming."

I nod and thank her, then I drive Sandy to Jeremy's tiny bungalow. He's watching his parents' two Chihuahua–Min Pin mixes, and Sandy races to the yard and starts rounding up the diminutive dogs.

"You're the only one I trust to take care of my dog," I remind Jeremy.

"That dog is in good hands."

"That dog catches Frisbees on the beach. Those are hard to come by."

Jeremy points to the tiny beasts in his yard. "*Those* dogs are not chick magnets. I take those dogs to the beach, and the girls want to take me shopping and ask which shoes to buy."

"My dog is a lady magnet," I say, and pat Jeremy on the back. "You will score endlessly with her by your side."

"I'm taking her to the pier every day."

"Take good care of her."

"I will. But I'm *not* sending you photos of her."

"But text me, okay? Let me know how Sandy is doing?"

He laughs and shakes his head. "You're embarrassing. You're like a girl when it comes to this dog."

"Don't be a sexist pig," I say.

"Get out of here, asshole."

I call Sandy over, rub her head, pet her ears, and tell her to be good. She tilts her head as if she's listening. Her tongue hangs out of her mouth. I tell her I love her in a voice so low Jeremy can't hear me say it.

Next, I go to Kate's home to say goodbye to my cousin.

She parks her hands on my shoulders and looks up, her eyes fierce. "Don't crash any cars or punch any walls in Tokyo. It'll be harder for me to come rescue you."

"I'll do my best to exercise self-restraint."

I take off for the law firm. I tell Don Jansen, the managing partner, he can reach me on my cell if he needs anything. That might be one of the most ridiculous things I've ever said to anyone.

"I'll do my best not to call," he says with a smile.

He won't call. He's never called me. Even when I interned here. Don's been running this place since Ian cut back his hours, then when he quit earlier this year. I might own the joint, but I'm not needed day in and day out. Don is.

He claps me on the shoulder. "Looking forward to seeing you here when you're back."

When I'm back—because I can't live in this in-between state forever.

That's why I'm leaving.

I say goodbye and head to the plane that'll take me 5,400 miles away. I'm ready to meet Kana, to see my brother's doctor, to learn the things I don't know.

When I sink into my seat in row twenty-three, Holland by my side, I'm not sure if this is real. Or maybe this is the new surreal direction that life after a hall pass has taken.

For the first time in weeks, I don't feel so alone.

14

Andrew

A body of water broke us up.

It's the largest and deepest one on earth, reaching its fingertips from the Arctic Ocean to Antarctica, from Asia and Australia to the Americas.

This 64-million-square-mile beast covers one-third of the earth, and that was more than enough to make Holland and me an impossibility three years ago.

I guess sometimes you want something so badly, you jump even if you know you'll crash. The jump was worth it, an exhilarating free fall, despite what was coming.

It's ironic that we're now crossing the Pacific together, but we're *not* together. Three years ago, I'd have given a million bucks, years off my life, or my right thumb for a way for us to stay together.

But that was the wide-eyed younger me—the one who had only experienced *one* seismic shift, not two.

Now, I take what I can get from Holland, and it's a strange new breed of companionship between us as we fly over the vast blue water while watching a spy movie set in space.

"It's so ridiculously unreal—all the CGI—that I love it to pieces," she says, waving at the seatback screens as she tugs out her earbuds.

"I don't think they could shoot it on a set," I say drily.

"Ya think?"

"Smartass."

"Same to you."

When the flick ends, we play cards, with Holland killing it at gin rummy.

"Card shark," I mutter.

She blows on her fingers.

When the meal arrives, she angles her phone above the tray full of rice and vegetables to snap a shot.

"What the hell are you doing?"

"For my Yelp review."

"You're really doing a Yelp review of airline food?"

"Absolutely. The only question is how many stars it'll earn." She spears a piece of wilted pepper and bites   it.   After   chewing,   she   declares, "Two-point-five."

"You're a harsh Yelper."

She smirks. "It's hilarious that you thought I'd really do that."

I set down my plastic fork, indignant. "The whole thing was a setup?"

She nods, proud of her ruse.

"See? You do take advantage of me."

Those words immediately evoke the other night. She locks eyes with me, and the joking ceases. Heat blazes across her irises, and a groan works its way up my chest. She's thinking the same thing, remembering the same moments I am. How we crashed into each other, all need and pent-up longing, how we nearly set the couch into flames. I can hear the sounds she made, feel how she moved. I see it all in her eyes, the images flashing like a film reel snapping. A hand on a face. Fingers laced through hair. Legs wrapped around hips. Lips parted. Eyes closed. Breath coming fast.

I'd watch that film again a thousand times over, even though it always ends the same.

We cut to black.

And now we're here, riding across the sky, knees brushing each other, the guy on the other side of me snoring.

"I don't take advantage of you," she whispers.

"I know you don't."

"I don't," she says again, firmer this time.

I'm firm too. "It was a joke."

"Okay," she says, like she's giving in.

"It was, Holland."

She plucks the in-flight magazine from the back of the seat and snaps it open. "Storytime," she declares, and then reads me an article. In Japanese. "What did you think?"

I scratch my jaw. "Considering I have hardly a clue what you said, how much of a disadvantage will I be at in Tokyo? I haven't been there in a few years."

She shoots me a look. "I'm aware of that."

Open mouth. Insert foot. That seems to be the stilted way we are today.

"It wasn't deliberate," I mutter.

She sighs then fixes on a smile. "It's okay. It was the decision we made. Besides, you couldn't just jet off to Tokyo whenever you wanted."

"And you couldn't just jet back to LA either," I toss back, because there's still room in my mouth for more of my foot.

"Anyway," she says, shifting gears, "you'll be fine. You studied it when you were younger, right?"

I nod. "My parents made us take classes as kids. I don't remember much though."

"I bet you'll pick up the language again quickly. It's there in your brain—it just needs to be dusted off. I'll help you as much as I can, especially since I don't start for another few weeks. By the way, what's first on your treasure map?"

I think about this for a minute. "Probably the teahouse. Have you been?"

She shakes her head. "No."

"Do you want to go with me?"

"Sure."

I feel like a kid in high school asking a girl out, since I don't have a clue what her response of *sure* means.

Then I remind myself—she's been crystal clear. She laid it out at my house over toast. We aren't a thing. We're not here as a couple. We're here as . . . sidekicks.

Explorers.

Adventurers.

We're Indiana Jones. Harry Potter. Star-Lord.

We're on a quest to understand my family.

It doesn't matter if we're awkward, if we rehash the past, if we tease, or if we don't.

We are only this, and no more.

* * *

I'm not tired when I file off the plane, pass through customs, and purchase two tickets for the train from the airport into the center of Tokyo. I'm not tired, either, when I sit on a red upholstered seat for the quick ride to the city center.

Holland is a different story. Her eyes start to flutter.

"You can rest your head on my shoulder," I tell her.

"I'm okay," she says on another huge yawn.

"Really, I won't bite."

"Maybe for just a minute." She lays her head on my shoulder, and I check my messages.

For a sliver of a second, I imagine Ian's written to me, like he did the weekend in April when I flew to Miami with some of my classmates for some pro bono work required for a course.

Ian: Don't forget sunscreen. And be sure to enjoy the view on South Beach. It's the land of beautiful people.

Andrew: I'll be trotting out my best pickup lines between helping the indigent with their legal needs.

Ian: No one ever suggested you had good pickup lines. ☺

Andrew: You're right. They all suck. Because I learned them from you.

Ian: As if I'd share my best material. BTW, love ya. Glad you made it safely.

Andrew: Back atcha. The love thing.

Ian: You can say it. C'mon. Serve it up to me.

Andrew: Fine. Love ya. Bye.

We'd made a promise when our parents died that we wouldn't forget to tell each other we gave a shit. I don't think we ever forgot to say we loved each other —in our way—when one of us traveled.

As the train rattles, a sharp sensation cuts through me, like a slice down my chest. This trip is the first time I've flown since he passed.

There are no messages from him waiting. There will never be another one, and the cut deepens as I read through some of our old texts. Sometimes, it's the little habits that are hardest to say goodbye to. Harder to break. Harder to mourn.

I close the thread before the cut smarts any more.

There's a message from someone else, and I need to tend to it. Holland's sound asleep on my shoulder as I open a text from my cousin.

Kate: Hope you landed safely! Keep me posted. Also, just a thought—maybe you want to move the date for your Bar exam? Happy to do that for you if I can!

I curse and run my hand through my hair. I fucking forgot. How did I forget to move it? I spent so much time in the spring studying for it, and then I stopped. There's no way I can take the Bar next month.

I start a reply, then stop mid-word when I remember the day I hit the car in front of my house on purpose. How dismissive I was to Kate when she tried to help. How numb I felt. How empty I was.

Even here, with Holland snoozing on my shoulder and my brother's favorite city mere miles away, I'm still closer to *that* version of me than I am to some brand-spanking-new iteration.

But I also have enough distance to know I don't have to be a douche to Kate.

I was definitely a douche to her that day, and probably on others too. Taking a breath, I reply.

Andrew: That would be awesome if you can reschedule the Bar. I completely forgot to do that, and I would be so grateful if you could work your supreme wizardry magic. Also, in case I haven't said this enough—I appreciate you for all you've done. Thanks. Love ya.

Kate: Thank you for saying that, and for letting me help. I love you too! More soon! xoxo

I close my phone and gaze out the window at the lush green fields we're passing in the suburbs, which soon turn into squat apartment buildings at the edge of the city, which then become skyscrapers and sleek, steel structures in the middle of Tokyo. The train arrives gently in Shibuya Station, and I rustle Holland, who stirs, sighs, and blinks.

"Hey. We're here."

She takes another deep breath but can't seem to shake off the sleepiness. I grab her suitcase from the rack and toss my lone backpack on my shoulder. I packed lightly, not wanting to bother with checked baggage. I stuffed everything I might need—laptop, shorts, T-shirts, some books, and a pair of flip-flops —into an oversized camping backpack. My sneakers are on my feet.

I roll her giant suitcase behind me as she ambles along by my side. It's strange to be helping her, since she knows this city so much better than I do.

The doors open, not with a screech but with a *whoosh*, and the crowds of people do not push or shove. They politely shuffle off. It's five-thirty in the evening on a Sunday night in June, and the station is bustling.

We push through the final turnstile at the Hachikō exit. We're at one of the busiest, craziest intersections in the world, because Shibuya Station sits at the convergence of a half dozen streets, where Holland took that selfie for me—a picture I love. I want to capture a new moment here, right now, three years later. Then I want to text it to her and tell her she doesn't have to miss me anymore, ever. She can have me. I'm here.

But it's just *for now*.

So there's no point in a *for now* selfie.

My hands remain at my sides, and instead, I watch her as she drinks in the view with wide eyes. "Home," she whispers, and it hits me like a fist in the solar plexus.

This is her place.

Her land.

I'm in a foreign city—no kidding—but this is her stomping ground.

I knew that, logically, but I didn't truly get it on a deeper level until this second.

I'm not her home. And her home doesn't include me.

"Look," she whispers reverently, pointing. "That was one of Ian's favorite things."

I turn and nod. "Yeah, it was."

Carved into the street-side wall of the subway

station is a bright, chunky mosaic of stars, rainbows, and a white Akita with a perfectly coiled tail. The story goes like this—the dog Hachikō followed his owner, a university professor, to work every morning and waited for his return in the evenings. One day in 1925, his master failed to show. He had died while teaching. But Hachikō was loyal to the end. The dog walked to the subway stop every day, waiting for the same train for the next several years until his own death.

I tap the dog's head once for good luck. Holland taps his chin. She gestures to the intersection. "I can walk you to your place."

"It's okay. I know how to get there. Go get some sleep."

As if on cue, she yawns again. "It's possible I might conk out. See you tomorrow?"

"I'll text you later to make plans."

Then I go one way, and she heads another.

Two directions.

Two lives.

Two apartments.

We're together, but we're not at all. Perhaps it'll always be this way.

I cross the intersection and join the sea of people fanning out in all directions.

I'm with all these people, but I'm still alone.

15

Andrew

I open the familiar glass-paneled door to the lobby of the apartment building that still feels more like Ian's than mine, even though it was ours, and press the elevator button.

The last time I was here was an impulsive trip the summer after my first year of law school.

The day classes ended, Ian surprised me by picking me up on campus, looking all cool and *Risky Business* with shades on. "We're getting out of town," he'd declared, smacking his palm on the shining red door of his car.

"Vegas, baby?"

He scowled. "Hell, no. We're flying far, far away. I

have a craving for fish, and I have credit card miles burning a hole in my pocket."

Enough said. We took off on a ten-hour flight across the sea and went to the fish market for breakfast the next morning.

"I'm going to OD on sushi," I'd said, patting my belly while pushing away the bowl of rice and fish at the food stall we loved.

"If you do, I'll revive you, so you can have some more."

"That sounds like a most excellent plan."

My stomach growls as the elevator rises, and I'm hungry from thinking about breakfast. I'll need fuel before I go to the teahouse tomorrow.

But as I imagine my first full day, something is missing, and it's the woman I just left. My instinct lately has been to go it alone, but if I'm here to figure out how the hell to be happy again, I ought to push past that gut impulse to fly solo. Kate wanted me to talk more; Jeremy encouraged me to hang out with friends.

I draw a steadying breath and send Holland a text.

Andrew: I'm already hungry for sushi. Fish market tomorrow?

I set my phone in my pocket as I reach the sixth floor and turn the key in the door of our—*my*, I need to get used to saying *my*, especially since I'm the one who has to decide what to do with it—apartment.

I pause as I wrap my hand around the knob, bracing to be clobbered by memories.

But when I open the door and step inside, it's like a deep inhale of fresh mountain air. This place is small—it *is* Tokyo real estate after all—but it *feels* big compared to my house in Los Angeles somehow.

More than that, it feels *alive*.

I drop my backpack by the door and turn into the kitchen, running my hand across the outside of the fridge, over the bright white sliver of the countertop, then along the panes of the window that look out to the busy street below.

I return to the living room, breathing in the familiar surroundings—the blond hardwood floors, the light-green couch, the bookshelves with the framed photos our parents left behind—all of us as kids, then the two of us, then a shot of Laini at her wedding. *Should I have told her I'd left the country?*

Nah. I'll mention it the next time she emails me.

I head into the second bedroom. There's only room for a low futon with a white mattress on hardwood slats and a slim three-drawer bureau. I hesitate again before I enter the room Ian used, unsure whether the ghosts from his life here will swallow me whole.

But for some reason, seeing the bed neatly made, like he did it at home, doesn't hurt. It feels strangely comforting, maybe even calming, to see he was the same here as he was there. That's the brother I know.

I close the door, and I'm about to head to the bathroom to inspect the medicine cabinet when I notice the entryway table tucked in the corner of the living room.

There's the World Series cap Kana mentioned in her note, the crossword puzzle books, a John Legend ticket stub from last fall, and a magnet from a bowling alley back home—Silverspinner Lanes. I pick it up, flip it over, but there's no secret code on it, no key to tell me why it's here. There's only a simple answer—he probably tossed it on the desk when emptying his pockets. But why was this in his pocket, especially while on an international flight?

I set it down and grab the stack of cards.

The first card is a picture of a black-and-white cat. I know instantly it's from Laini. She always loved tuxedo cats.

Dear Ian,

So glad we did that!! xoxo

Love, Laini

Did what? What did she do with Ian? She never mentioned the visit in her emails to me, and I hardly talked to her at the memorial service. I hardly talked to anyone at the service.

Under that card is another one, with a photo of a serene tropical beach on the front. Inside it is a sheet of stationery.

I unfold the paper and read.

Ian—you're probably too old for this, but we left you money anyway. Don't ONLY order pizza when we're gone in Hawaii! Get salads and veggies too! And look out for Andrew. Summer before college and all that—make sure he throws ZERO parties at the house! Also, we love you both so very much.

P.S. Did I mention to look out for Andrew? That boy is our troublemaker.

Love,
Anna and John
better known as . . .
Mom and Dad

I lean back in the chair and laugh at the word *trouble-maker*. I was their second straight A student, and I threw zero parties in high school. I smile widely, picturing my mom writing this note to her twenty-two-year-old son, telling him to look after her eigh-teen-year-old.

Maybe this letter should make me sad, but it doesn't. I like the humor, and the unsuccessful direc-tive to eat veggies.

I didn't eat a single stalk of broccoli when they were gone, and I have no regrets over the lack of greens that week.

I set down the note, wondering briefly why Ian brought these bits and pieces of his life to Tokyo.

My eyes drift to a framed photo on the corner of the table. It's Ian and Kana posing in front of a temple, his arm wrapped around her shoulder. Hers is tight around his waist. He wears the World Series cap—it's the photo mentioned in the letter. He still looks well. Or, well enough.

When I pick up the Lucite frame to peer at it more closely, I feel more photos behind it. Sliding them out, I flick through the shots of Ian and Kana around the city, then I freeze.

Holland gazes back at me, walking away from the camera, her hair blowing in the breeze, but she looks over her shoulder at the lens. A smile has started on her face, as if the photographer captured her unexpectedly—unexpectedly laughing, smiling. She's in a park near a cherry blossom tree.

I turn to the next shot. It's Holland too, in a different outfit, shrugging happily as if to say, "Fine, take my picture outside this pachinko parlor."

The last shot of her mocks me too. It's a close-up of her face. She's holding a mic, singing at a karaoke bar.

My fingers shake, and my stomach churns.

Why the hell does my brother have these shots of my ex-fucking-girlfriend hidden behind the pictures of his girlfriend? He never told me he spent so much time with Holland here.

She neglected to mention that little fact too.

Even when I asked her the night we kissed at my house.

I jam my hand through my hair, remembering the words she'd said before we tumbled onto my couch, grinding against each other.

He wasn't there to see me—he was there to see her.

But he did see her.

He saw her often, it seems. I remember, too, the tears in Holland's eyes after she read Kana's letter. Other memories pop up like in a Whac-a-Mole game. Holland reading a book to Ian. Holland at the house for hospice care.

I try to whack them away. But they mock me.

Seething, I stare at the snapshots, burning holes in them with my eyes.

I drop the photos and walk away. I can't believe this. I refuse to believe what my mind is trying to make of these things.

No, just fucking no.

There's no fucking way.

I pace, shoveling my hand through my hair as I try to apply all my skills to this evidence like a good lawyer would.

There is no evidence of contact. There is no evidence of love. There is no evidence of anything more than friendship.

These are only snapshots, and the best-case scenario is she hung out with Kana and Ian.

The worst case is . . .

I curse, grab my phone, and call Holland. It goes straight to voicemail. She must be down for the count.

I sink onto the couch so I can talk myself off the ledge, and a yawn seems to overtake me out of nowhere. I rub my eyes, and I turn, looking for the familiar face—black fur, curious brown eyes, a soft snout. Sandy always knows how to talk me down with her silence.

But my shrink isn't here.

Closing my eyes, I try to imagine she's here, and I present calm, logical, rational answers to her.

But even as I voice them—*just friends, just hanging out, just a group thing*—another voice gnaws away at my gut.

Is this why she stopped us from going further the other night? Is my brother's death hitting her more than she let on because they were a thing? Is that why she was out here working then came back to Los Angeles? Is Kana a fucking cover-up? Has it all been one massive secret between the two of them?

"No," I mutter, trying to calm my tired and racing brain. "Just fucking no. Don't go there."

I pinch the bridge of my nose, hard, to push the dangerous thoughts away.

But it's too late. They're boring into me, drilling their awfulness into my skull with cruel jack-hammers.

I need to focus on what matters—why I'm here.

I stand, roll my shoulders, exhale.

Shake it off.

I stalk to the bathroom and yank open the medicine cabinet. Jet lag is kicking in quickly, threatening to smother me in sleep. Bleary-eyed, I reach for a prescription bottle. It's a cancer drug, and it's barely been touched. There's another kind next to it. This one was marked "open" on Kana's list, but it looks like nearly all the pills are still in the bottle, like Ian hardly took any. I know these drugs by heart, know their side effects and their benefits.

What I don't know is why they're full. Is it door one, two, or three? I imagine a logic problem, and I try to puzzle it out, but the answer is still blurry because there are pieces of my brother I don't know.

I grab another bottle. It's Percocet, and it was filled by a pharmacy here several months ago. But even in my sleepy state, I can tell that none have been taken either.

My pulse spikes. My mouth waters.

My brain begs me—*please turn me off*.

I don't want to go there, but I don't want to stay in this threadbare state. Logic has flown the coop and left only a dark wasteland in its place.

Besides, perhaps this is a gift from beyond, a beautiful parting gift indeed, because these work wonders on the living. I open the cap and free one of the beauties. I put the pill on my tongue and it feels like blasphemy—taking my brother's painkillers when he was in real pain. But I do it anyway, swallowing it dry. Once it's down, I take another. Two will work faster.

I return to the living room, flop down on the couch, and let sleep pull me under.

When I rise, I check my phone, and a message from Holland tells me she'd love to meet me at the fish market.

I don't reply. I don't know how.

I don't know if I really want to anymore.

16

Andrew

The doctor is in.

Or the doctor isn't in.

Or the doctor isn't in yet.

See, I don't know, because there isn't any sign on his door. There isn't an OPEN or CLOSED sign. Or a BACK SOON sign. Or a Post-it note letting the next-of-kin of his former patient know where to find Dr. Takahashi, the doctor who gave orders to drink tea.

I tracked down his number and called his office before I flew here. I left a message and asked for an appointment three days ago.

It's past nine, so I knock harder, as if the answers will come when it hurts enough. My knuckles are red and worn now, and still, no one opens the door.

Once again, I find myself without a decoder ring, same as last night with the letters, and the mementos, and the photos.

Ian left a few clues behind, like at a dinner-party murder mystery game. But without the official answer key, I'm jumping to conclusions.

I wince, remembering last night and the terrible ones I jumped to.

I lower my fist, sigh, and leave the doctor's building with no more information than I had when I started.

This is getting to be a pattern with me.

I catch the subway and walk along the edge of the Tsukiji Fish Market, the largest fish market in the world. I can hear the merchants inside, sloshing around in their knee-high boots in the fishy water that puddles on the concrete floor as they peddle everything from mackerel to eel to shrimp to salmon to tuna.

In the light of day, the things I thought last night so clearly can't be true. I feel ashamed and disloyal for even going there.

I reach the block of food stalls on the outskirts of the market and easily find the one my brother and I went to. I grab a stool and order a bowl of tuna and rice.

As I wait, I realize this much. My brother took me here—*this very place*—for fun.

He flew me across the sea to hang out with him

for the weekend. There's no way those photos of Holland mean there was anything between them.

I grab my phone and finally reply to her, telling her I'm at the food stalls.

Then I let last night's nightmare go, as a hunched-over Japanese woman slides a bowl in front of me. She returns to stirring a vat of miso soup.

I eat, savoring the food. My chopsticks dive into the bowl again, scooping up another heaping spoonful of rice and soy sauce and raw fish.

"Hey."

I look up and see a guy I know. "Hey, Mike."

He smiles and reaches over the counter to smack my arm.

He's my age, and he worked here the last time I visited. He was into music, always playing some cool Japanese tunes on low on his little stereo while he served up fish. We'd sometimes trade song recommendations. His English is perfect, and I remember that from being here—most people our age know English well.

"How's it going, man? I remember you. Ian's brother, right? Andrew?"

I'm glad he remembers me and that I don't have to dive into a lengthy explanation or reminder. "Yeah, I'm just here for—" I stop for a second. *To see if I can ever be happy, or even remotely human, again. Would you happen to have the magic cure?* "To see Tokyo again."

"How's Ian doing?"

There it is. That all-too-familiar moment when I have to tell someone, and we all become uncomfortable.

"Actually, he died last month," I say, clunky and awkward. Maybe it always will be.

Then the look. The tilt of the head, the heavy *oh*, like he's said the wrong thing. "Oh, man. I'm really sorry to hear that."

"Thanks."

"Damn, I'll miss him. He was here every day when he was in town."

"Yeah, he dug this place."

"He did." He pauses, a thoughtful look in his eyes. "How are *you* doing?" he asks.

The question startles me. Strangers rarely ask. "I'm okay," I say, and it feels true. I decide to test out more honesty—the simple kind. "I was supposed to take the bar next month, but I'm not. I pushed it off, and I'm glad I did."

Mike grabs a ceramic mug of tea from behind the counter and raises it high. "That deserves a toast."

I lift my tea mug and clink. "It does?"

He nods intensely. "You're taking a stand against the tyranny of tests."

I laugh. "I'm not entirely sure that's what it means, since I won't be able to practice law without it."

Mike wiggles his fingers. "Work with me here, man. You're an anarchist."

I laugh some more and take a gulp of the hot beverage. "To anarchy."

He puts down his cup, grabs a blade, and pulls some fish onto a cutting board. "Speaking of anarchy, did you hear this new band, the Anarchist Sages?"

Before I know it, I have a list of new bands to check out, and he has the same from me.

"Thanks, Mike. It's good to have new tunes as I rebel against the tyranny of tests."

He points his knife at me in a *you know it* gesture. "And you'll need a playlist for the ladies too. Don't forget the ladies."

"I could never forget the girl." Singular, not plural.

He slices a piece of tuna. "Your brother was like that too. He was here with his girl a lot. I told him it was radically unfair that he snagged the prettiest Japanese girl around and didn't give the local men a shot."

I laugh, and it feels damn good because I can picture Ian's reaction to that comment. A what-can-you-do shrug, paired with a slightly cocky smile.

"She's a nice gal," Mike adds as he works the blade through another fish. "So was your sister."

My chopsticks clatter to the wood counter, as I stumble across the dossier to one of the murder mystery clues—the connection to the postcard on the desk. The trouble is, a searing pang of jealousy pounds into me, thinking Laini might have known why Ian was here, why he wasn't taking his meds, maybe even why he sought alternative treatments.

"When was my sister here?" The words feel bitter.

Mike looks up for a second. "A few months back? Maybe January, maybe February?"

"That's great," I say to Mike, but it's a lie. It's not great that I thought I knew my brother better than anyone. Now I feel like he's slipping further away from me.

Mike turns to take an order from another customer, and I glance down at the remains of my rice and fish.

"I'll have what he's having."

I look up to see Holland.

17

Holland

His eyes are edged with hurt, but not the kind I saw in Los Angeles. This is different. Not as painful. More like a surprised kind of hurt, and I'm not sure how to read him, or what's gone into this new emotional cocktail.

But then he says, "You found me," and his tone seems even, so I keep mine even too, so I can try to figure out where he's at.

"I'm a huntress." I take the seat next to him and say hello to the guy behind the counter. "Also, I thought you'd be at this food stall when you said *the* food stalls."

"It's the best one here," he says, but his response is far too one-note for my liking. Something is amiss.

I ease into the conversation. "Did you win the fight against jet lag last night, or did it take you down too?"

"It definitely pulled me under." He takes a bite of his food, then tips his chin at me. "You crashed hard last night."

Maybe he's just adjusting to the time zone. "Jet lag, one. Holland, zero. I was down for the count as soon as I reached my apartment. Sorry I wasn't around."

"It's no biggie. I get it."

"What did you do last night? Pachinko parlor? Karaoke? Late-night clubbing?" I ask, tossing out ridiculous options.

He winces and looks away, muttering, "Stayed at the apartment. Looked through some stuff."

"What did you find, oh treasure hunter?" I ask curiously, wondering if he unearthed some memento of Ian's that pierced his heart. It can't have been easy being alone in that place for the first time. I would have offered to stay with him, but I'm not sure that would have truly helped either one of us. Close quarters would be far too tempting for me.

He takes his time answering, the words coming out sharper, bordering on suspicious. "Photos, letters, and pictures of you I found behind a framed photo of Kana. Three pictures of you, to be exact."

I tilt my head, processing this news—news I don't entirely like hearing. "Exact, indeed." My hackles are raised, and I arch a brow. "And where were the photos taken?"

"In the park or something. Another was at karaoke."

I furrow my brow, trying to remember those times. They feel vaguely familiar. "A park sounds like someplace I was once," I tease, trying to diffuse the situation.

"What did you guys do together?" Andrew's voice is strained, and his face is anguished now.

And I officially know why he's off today, why his mood has been too even. He's holding something in, and he's thinking something he shouldn't be thinking whatsoever.

A plume of righteous anger rises in me. I don't let it burn me, but I won't let him tread in these dangerous territories. Not only for his sake, but for mine too, because I won't bear this burden. I hold up a hand. "Don't go there."

"Go where?"

I shake my head, keeping calm. Inside, I'm wound tight, because I *know* where his brain has traveled, and he's so insanely wrong. "Be careful before you say anything."

He licks his lips. "What do you think I'm going to say?"

I straighten my shoulders. "I don't know, but I think if you do go someplace dangerous, you'll regret it."

He squeezes his eyes shut. His Adam's apple bobs as he swallows, like it hurts. "I'm sorry."

The rawness in his voice hooks into me, and there's a part of me that's proud of him for not saying more. There's a part that's pissed, though, that he even let himself think the worst—of his brother and of me.

No wonder he looked guilty.

I soften. *Slightly.* "Why don't you ask me about those times?"

He sighs heavily. "What did you do with Ian when he was here?"

The question is so needy, so honest, that I understand why he hurts. He wants to know his brother, and he wants to know me.

"I hung out with him and Kana. I loved your brother—don't you get that?"

"I do get that. Trust me, I do."

As he stares at the woman stirring the vat of soup, I catalog the features I know well: his cheekbones, his strong nose, his square jaw. His lips I love. "But do you want to know what we talked about?"

He turns to look at me. "What did you talk about?"

I point to him. "You."

He smiles, a childlike wonder in his expression, a flicker of home-brewed happiness in his deep brown eyes. "Yeah?"

"I asked him about you. He told me stories of

you. We talked about you. So before you start thinking stupid things, think better of your brother. Think better of me." I squeeze his hand. He squeezes back.

"I do. I do think better of you, and of him. Sometimes I'm just a fucking mess." He shrugs. "Forgive me?"

I smirk. "I forgave you when you had the guts to not say it."

"Good. That's good. Glad I shut my trap at the right moment."

I reach for his arm, set my palm on it. It's hard for me to not touch him. "He had a life here. He loved Kana. And I loved him—as a friend, and only ever as a friend. And we did things together. I don't know why those pictures are behind the frame, but I know this: you were never far from his mind, or mine."

"I'm an asshole."

"Are you though?"

"Am I?"

I look him over, as if I'm appraising him. "I think you're a step or two away from it. There's a thin line between almost and asshole."

He laughs. "I'd like to not cross that line."

"You're doing okay so far."

He wipes his hand across his brow in relief. "Whew."

The guy behind the counter asks Andrew if he wants more tea.

"That'd be great. Thanks, Mike." Andrew turns to me and lowers his voice. "Mike mentioned my sister came to visit Ian. Neither one of them ever told me about it."

I pat his arm and shoot him a smile. "If it makes you feel any better, neither one of them told me either."

He laughs. "A little better."

Mike slides him the tea. "Here you go." He tips his chin to me. "Do you need anything else . . .?" He trails off like he's waiting for my name.

"I'm Holland." I offer my hand.

He shakes. "I'm Mike. And it's nice to meet Andrew's girl." He wiggles his eyebrows at Andrew and returns to his food prep.

I don't correct him. I'm not his girl. But in many ways, I suppose I am.

Instead, I tell Andrew, "You should reach out to your sister and ask her."

"I should, and I will."

Mike hands me the fish and rice bowl, and I thank him.

* * *

We wander through the market, stopping in little stalls selling teacups and chopsticks, plates and fans.

Andrew points to a display of sapphire-blue square plates in every size from about one square inch to large enough to hold two Thanksgiving turkeys.

"This." He lifts the tiniest one. "Is this for when I'm not very hungry but just want, say, one blueberry?"

I laugh and grab the next size up. "This is obviously for a pat of butter."

"But just one pat," he says in mock seriousness.

"Of course. With one of those cool scalloped designs in it."

"Do you ever wonder how someone learns to do that?"

"Become a butter sculptor? I've actually never thought about that. Do you think you need to go to art school?"

"Probably, unless there are butter sculptor schools."

"I suspect the butter sculpting academies also teach ice sculpture."

We meander into the next stall and check out the vast array of fans. As I flick open a pastel-green one with a sparrow design, I turn to him, fanning my face. "Should I get a parasol to go with it?"

"Yes, and then try and use both with a straight face."

"That would be impossible."

We make our way around the shopping area, like we're exploring together. Which we are, and we aren't. Tokyo is foreign to me, yet it's also my home.

But here with Andrew, the man I once wanted to see the world with, this feels like something we were always meant to do.

Something we once daydreamed about.

One afternoon during the summer we were together, I was lolling around in his pool, floating on a raft as I glided over to him. He hung by the side of the water, elbows on the ledge, sunglasses on because it was high noon, with the kind of heat that made you feel like you'd been baking from the inside out. I pushed his shades on top of his head and said, "Let's go to Fiji."

"Let's go to Tahiti."

"Bali."

"How about the Cook Islands? It's practically off the map."

"The Maldives."

"Seychelles."

I splashed water on him. "Now you're just showing off."

"The Maldives? I think you might be showing off too."

"I was just trying to impress you. Geography was my best subject. I can totally name all fifty states. Just try me."

He pulled me off the raft and brought me up against his hot, hard body. "It'll make me want you even more," he joked, even though he seemed to want me a helluva lot right then.

"Do you know how long I've liked you, Andrew Peterson?"

"No. How long?"

I spread my arms as wide as they could go. "This long."

"That's a long time to harbor a crush, Holland St. James."

My nerves skittered, but I kept them at bay. I was going to say the word—the word that was so hard to say when real life gave us a timeline that my heart didn't want to match. The word that meant everything.

"Not just a crush, Andrew. I'm in love with you."

He smiled, slow and happy, his eyes sparkling. "I'm so in love with you."

The guy I loved, loved me. My greatest dream was coming true. My greatest dream would soon end, since I was going away, but in that moment, I let myself revel in the bliss. "I've been in love with you for so long."

We kissed gently, and we kissed feverishly, and when we pulled apart, his hands were on my hips, my bikini top was gone, and we were about to figure out if pool sex would work. "I want to go to all those places with you."

"I'll take you there. I'll take you wherever you want to go."

"Take me anywhere, Andrew."

Now, here we are, *anywhere*.

The memory rushes over me, spilling into the present, mingling with who we are now, on the other side of pain.

We're those same people, but we're so very different too.

And still, we're talking, joking, teasing, wandering, figuring things out. We're *anywhere* together, and for a few moments, this feels like part of the healing.

It's a healing we both need—from the years apart. From the number that time and distance did on our one-time greatest dreams.

We explore more stalls then wind up on the outskirts of the market where vending machines line the concrete walls. I stop at one peddling mango, pineapple, and grape chewy candy.

"I love these," I say as I peruse the offerings.

"Let me guess. Grape?"

Nodding, I reach into my pocket for change.

He wraps his hand over mine and shakes his head. "Allow me. A gentleman always pays for vending machine candy."

"Ooh, that is the height of chivalry."

I drop the unused coins back into my jeans pocket while he slides in some money and punches the button for the grape Hi-Chews.

I grab the packet and unwrap the end, handing him one. "Peace offering."

He pops it in his mouth. "Yum. I like it when you *come* in peace."

My eyebrows rise. "Naughty," I whisper.

"Who me?" He adopts an I'm-so-innocent look.

"You know you are," I say. I should stop grinning, but I can't.

He smiles too, but then as he stares at me, the smile disappears. His eyes darken, and he moves closer. "I don't feel like the strong one right now."

Butterflies sweep through me, thrilling and scary. "Why aren't you strong?"

His gaze locks with mine. "I need you to know, Holland, that I thought about you all the time. It was so hard when you left, and then you came back, and now you're here in front of me. And when we kissed the other night, it felt like the only thing that made sense in the world. Do you know that?"

"I could tell when you were kissing me," I whisper as I lean against the machine, his words sending my pulse racing, my hopes bursting free.

"But every now and then, other things make sense. Talking to Mike, walking through the fish market, messaging Kate ..."

A light goes on in my chest, and my heart glows. I've needed this desperately—to know he has other routes to happiness that don't go through me. I don't want to be his crutch. I want to be a choice he makes freely, not a desperate second chance he's clinging to. "That makes me happy. I want other things to make sense for you too."

"They're starting to." He points to the packet of grape candy in my hand. "Like this candy."

"I love that candy."

His eyes sweep over me then lock with mine. "But you—you still make the most sense."

My heart soars so high, so near to the edge of the atmosphere, I worry it'll escape.

Because I know what he's saying. We're saying the word *love* without saying the word.

I drop the candy in my pocket, then raise a hand to reach for his shirt. "You make the most sense to me too." I grab the fabric and pull him near, the wish to get closer to him blotting out my worries. "I'm not the strong one either. Forgive me for this moment of weakness."

"It's already granted," he whispers as I bring those lips I love to mine.

I breathe him in and let his warmth spread through me. His kisses undo me. They weaken my knees. They flutter my heart.

I never knew a kiss could turn me upside down. But with Andrew, it feels like light and stars and hope and sex and love and all the moments I want to get lost in. It feels like flying, and I don't want to land.

His lips trace mine, and I swear I'm soaring with open wings now.

I wrap my arms around his neck and bring him close, loving, just loving the feel of his body against mine. It's mind-bending, unraveling, and I wish I could understand it, list out the elements that make me melt.

But the *why* can't be duplicated—he kisses me like he loves me *and* like he's in love with me.

That's also why we have to stop. Our connection —for now—is fueled by a ragged need. He's not ready for us again. He could lose himself in us, like we're the Bermuda Triangle. As for me, my own desire to heal him is too consuming. It'll consume me if I don't take it slowly.

I remember some of Ian's last words to me.

"He still loves you so much it hurts him. Give him time."

I break the kiss, my hands on his chest, my breath coming fast.

His eyes are wild and hungry as he cups my cheek. "I'm not the stronger one, Holland."

"Then I'll have to be." I peel his hand off my face and thread my fingers through his. "Let's go see Kana."

He needs that more than he needs more of my lips.

18

Andrew

On the subway, Holland's busy reading a book on her phone, so I write an email to my sister. While primal instinct tells me to cut straight to the point, I rein that in. There's a card from her in the pile on Ian's desk here—it meant something to my brother. And if she came to visit him, I need to break out my best cordial self. Besides, she's emailed me every week since the service, and every week before for the last few months. They're short notes—mostly she checks in, or sends an internet meme. Usually, I've seen them already, so I respond with a word or two. Sometimes a sentence.

Hey Laini,

Hope you're well and the kids and hubby are good. I trust everyone is busy in your neck of the woods. I'm in Japan right now. I needed to get away from LA, so I'm taking care of some things here. I heard you saw Ian earlier in the year. Would love to hear more. Call me or email me back.

Andrew

I hit send, rewarding myself with not-even-an-asshole-at-all points, when my phone buzzes instantly. *That's fast.* But the reply's not from her.

I click open the text from Jeremy, and a photo fills the screen. The shot is of a pretty brunette wearing a gray V-neck T-shirt and board shorts, her hand resting on top of a dog's head. *My* dog. Sandy's looking the other way, but I can see half of her furry face. I laugh as I read the text.

Jeremy: This is Callie. I met her at the beach last night. Guess what? She loves dogs! Who woulda thunk it?

Jeremy: Also, for the record, I am not, technically, sending you a photo of your dog. I am sending you a photo of a babe.

I bang out a reply.

Andrew: For the record, I'm not thanking you for the photo that happens to include a head of a dog. I'm thanking you for where that woman's hand was when you took that picture.

I bump my shoulder to Holland's and show her the picture. She pretends to pet the dog's head through the screen. "What are you up to, Sandy?" she asks the screen.

God, I fucking love her.

The dog, and the woman.

* * *

When we reach Shibuya again, the nerves kick in. "I feel like I've been called into the principal's office."

"Do you think you'll wind up in detention?"

"I don't know what to expect when I talk to

Kana," I admit as we pass an electronics store where a salesman hawks a TV set.

"What do you most want to ask her?" Holland asks. The midday rush is full of men and women in business suits, mingled with über-trendy girls who *click-clack* down the sidewalks in chunky boots and playing-card earrings and dudes who wear plaid pants and sport dyed-blond hair. I try to picture Ian and Kana here on a weekday afternoon, weaving their way through these crowds.

I squint, but I can't quite see it. That's why I want to talk to her. I want to know him better.

But I hardly know her. We've talked briefly on the phone a few times, but that's all. When she came to visit Ian one weekend in the spring, I was in Miami for pro bono work, so I never met the woman who captivated him.

"I want to fill in the puzzle. I want to know what he was like when he was here. Why he was so joyful." I tilt my head, considering the possibilities. "Hell, maybe it's patently obvious. He was probably happy because he was getting laid."

Holland laughs, her hand on her belly as we pass a boba tea shop. "Sex *is* a natural pain reliever."

An image of the unopened bottle of Percocet flashes before me. Correction—*opened*. By me. A slash of guilt cuts through me, but I tell myself I can stop. I will stop.

Hell, maybe that's why Ian stopped taking

his meds.

"Endorphins, right?" I ask, as much to take my mind off the topic as to keep the conversation moving.

"Sex increases the production of oxytocin, the love hormone. It's released from the brain before climax, along with endorphins, which are a natural painkiller. Make sense?"

I scratch my jaw. "I'm not sure." I wiggle my eyebrows. "I feel like I'd do better with a hands-on tutorial."

She swats my elbow. "Oh, stop."

"No, I mean it."

"I know you mean it."

"I'm just saying, there's no substitute for experience."

She arches a brow as we near an intersection. "I think we both know what would happen if we embarked on that field trip."

We stop at the light, and I look her in the eyes. "What would happen?"

She answers matter-of-factly. "We'd never leave the bedroom."

I groan at the images flickering before my eyes. Holland stripping off the yellow T-shirt she's wearing, sliding out of those jeans, peeling off her panties. "I'd be fine with that. Also, thanks a lot for putting those ideas in my head right before I meet my brother's girl."

"I suspect you had them in your head already," she says, then gives me a flirty look.

She's flirtier over here, and I half wonder if it's something in the water, or if it's the escape from Los Angeles, a city that had become the epicenter of so much loss in my life.

I wink at her, since I like the flirty zone—it's a happy place, and that's where I'd like to be. "That is true. Those ideas are pretty much always present, especially after you launched yourself at me this morning in front of the vending machine."

Her eyes widen. "It was a mutual launch."

"All systems were go."

She points to the small park across the street. "Also, there she is."

I follow her gesture to find a woman tossing scraps of bread to squirrels.

"She's a squirrel feeder," I say in wonder as I see Kana in the flesh for the first time.

"Just like us," Holland adds quietly. "Only a different launch pad."

Instantly, I catalog the woman, as if her appearance will unlock clues. Red buckle shoes prop her up a few inches taller, and her purple blouse ripples in the breeze. She wears a short black skirt, pleated and a little playful. She fits in so well with this city— colorful, but not outrageous.

Holland shouts to her in Japanese, saying "Hey girl," I think.

As the dark-haired woman turns, the moment slows to a surreal crawl, and that's my fault because I've invested it with so much, like Kana is a vessel for all the secrets of the universe. Or mine, at least.

But now I see she's just a woman a few years older than we are, who's feeding wildlife in a city park.

Time speeds up when she waves back, then ticks faster as she sees me. We close the distance, but she's speedier, walking to me, her brown eyes wide and earnest, her lips curved into a smile.

Before she can say a word, and before I can mouth an awkward *hello*, her arms are around me.

"It's so good to finally meet you." It sounds like it's as much of a relief for her as it is for me. As if she needed this too.

Like that, the weirdness disappears.

We separate, and Holland says, "Guess I don't really need to introduce you two."

"I feel like I know you," Kana says to me, with only a trace of an accent. I remember Ian telling me she went to college in the United States and lived in San Francisco for a few years before returning to her home.

"It's good to meet you," I say, since I can't really say the same—I don't know her at all. But I want to know her better.

"Come. Sit." Kana points to the park bench. "We can chat."

Holland waves goodbye.

"You're leaving?" I ask her.

She smiles. "You guys don't need me."

And I suppose she's right. If she stayed, she'd be a safety net, and this isn't about her.

"I'll see you later?" I hope so.

She mimes typing on her phone. "You know where to find me."

Holland walks away, and I watch her for a few seconds, her bright blonde hair a contrast to the rest of the city.

"You look like Ian," Kana says.

"People usually say that."

"But he was better looking."

I crack up at her dry humor. "Can't say it's a bad thing that you think that."

She smiles again, and it's a warm, winning kind of grin. "I'm so sorry we never met before, but I want to let you know, if you need anything while you're in town, I'll do everything I can to help."

I rub my palms on the fabric of my shorts. "Thanks. I'm not sure what I need."

"How long are you here?"

I glance up at the sky as if the answer is in the clouds. "I'm here for as long as I have to be, I guess."

She smiles softly. "I understand. You want to know the sides of Ian you feel you didn't know."

"Yes."

"I'm not sure I had a special view into him, but I'll do what I can to share."

Since she's being so direct, I cut to the chase. "What do you know about the meds? Did he stop taking them?"

She offers a rueful smile, and in it, I sense she's about to tell me some sad truth. "I didn't keep track of that," she says, surprising me. "We honestly didn't talk that much about his illness."

That's not what I expected to hear. "You didn't?"

She shakes her head, runs her slim fingers through her thick black hair. "We talked about a million other things. We talked about music, and the best type of soba noodles. We talked about books, and whether mango boba tea was better than milk tea. We talked about baseball, and he tried valiantly, even until the bitter end, to convince me the Dodgers were the greatest." She leans back on the bench, her eyes far away for a moment, then she meets my gaze. "But I remained loyal to my Tokyo Giants."

"And he remained ever loyal to the Dodgers."

"And he liked to come see me play."

"Play? Baseball?" I furrow my brow.

She laughs, shaking her head. "Don't I wish I could hit a fastball? No, he came to see my blues band. I play saxophone with some friends, and he'd watch me perform, and afterward, we'd drink tea, or eat mochi ice cream, or track down a noodle shop as we walked around the city at night."

I picture the two of them, and now I can see it. What was blurry moments ago is clearer. My brother was just a guy seeing a girl in her hometown.

"Sounds a lot like dating," I deadpan.

She laughs. "Yes, it was exactly like dating."

"He was here a lot," I say, fishing around for something, but I'm not sure what exactly.

"He was, and yet it felt like never quite enough."

Those words hit me in the gut. That's how it goes when you lose someone you love—you feel as if you never had enough time, enough memories with them.

Then again, I had more moments with Ian than anyone else was lucky enough to have. There's no one on earth who amassed more hours with the guy than I did.

And yet, what I wouldn't give for another day.

Another ball game to cheer at.

Another chance to dunk his head underwater in the pool. And to be dunked.

Another pizza and a movie night.

My throat tightens, but I push my way through, returning my focus to Kana, who also wanted more time.

"Were you in love with him?" Maybe it's strange to ask. Maybe it's fucking obvious. All signs point to yes. But even so, I want to hear from her.

Her smile is soft, and her eyes are true. "Very much so."

It's not that I doubted that she loved him, but Kana has always been abstract to me. She's someone Ian talked about from time to time. She's someone he visited. But she hasn't been entirely real to me.

Until now.

I'm not the one to give comfort, but it feels like an affront to the universe if I don't let *her* know how much she mattered to him. "He felt the same way about you."

She nods and whispers a quiet *thank you*.

But dating, and loving, involves harder stuff too. I clear my throat, pushing past the prying nature of the question I need to ask. "May I ask if you went with him to his appointments and stuff? Like Dr. Takahashi?"

"I did, but Ian didn't see him every time he was here. He saw him perhaps a half dozen times," she says. That's another puzzle piece, but I can't quite slide it in. I don't know if a handful of appointments means Takahashi was a voodoo doctor or something else. "He brought me along because he loved to spend time in the Asakusa district of town, where the doctor is, and he wanted to share it with me."

"He did?"

She smiles. "After his appointments, we'd walk through the nearby shopping arcade. You know the kind that sells fans and little cat statues with the waving arms?"

She mimes the movement, and I nod.

"And we'd grab chocolate-dipped biscuits or jelly crepes. He liked to joke that it was a good thing the doctor was located in such a cool area."

"I need to see the doctor. I left him a message a few days ago. But I went there today, and there was no answer."

"Oh," Kana says, her expression turning sad.

"What's that for?"

She winces as if she has bad news. But I can handle bad news. It's what I do. "He's in Tibet for a few weeks. I came to know one of the ladies who works there, a receptionist. She mentioned it to me during one of Ian's appointments while I was waiting for him. The doctor treats the indigent for no charge for a month every summer."

"He'll be gone for a few weeks?"

She nods.

I sigh heavily then shrug. "I guess that means I won't see him for a few weeks, then."

She flashes a smile. "Tokyo is not a bad place to pass the time. I'll be working, but I'm happy to show you around when I can. Maybe to see some of Ian's favorite places?"

She's an angel. "I would love that." Feeling a bit like a cartoon character batting his or her eyes, I ask, "Can you take me to the teahouse?"

"Yes, but it's closed right now. Would you want to meet again on Wednesday to go?"

I would love to. That's another step closer to

knowing Ian better. Already, I've learned the person who drew my brother to this side of the world is exactly the kind of woman I'm glad he spent his final year with—one who is passionate, kind, and loving.

That's a damn good thing to uncover.

Even so, a tinge of sadness hangs over me as I look back on the last few months I had with him. I was so damn busy with school. Hell, he'd wanted me to stay busy. He'd urged me to focus on classes.

And I still wish . . . I still fucking regret that I didn't toss out the final semester and finish law school another time.

Ian would have killed me if I'd done that, though, and that thought makes me laugh out loud.

Kana smiles curiously. "Everything okay?"

"I was just thinking how I wish I had ditched all my classes last semester to hang out with Ian more."

She cracks up. "As if he would have permitted that."

I crack up too, picturing the look on his face. "Yeah, you're right. He would have won that battle."

"He definitely would have won that battle. In fact, I think he did."

"He got what he wanted."

"You finished."

I nod, smiling. "I did. *He* wanted that."

And maybe that's more important than what *I* wanted.

19

Andrew

The next morning is different.

I know what to say to Holland when I wake up.

Andrew: What's on the agenda today, tour guide?

Holland: I'm your tour guide now?

Andrew: Um, yeah. Hello? Sidekick duties call.

Holland: Oh, but of course. Part of sidekick duties includes serving as your tour guide. Let me go check the TripAdvisor in my brain.

Andrew: It's right next to your Yelp reviews.

Holland: It is! Let's see . . . I need to pick up a few things for my apartment, so we could run errands or . . .

Andrew: I love errands. But I like the "or" better.

Holland: Meet me at the station in thirty minutes.

I like this option, and I don't even know what it is.

* * *

We exit Nakameguro Station, and after one block, we're walking through a quiet residential area of the city.

"This is unexpected," I say.

Holland nods excitedly. "One of my former co-workers lives here. She invited me to dinner last year, and I'd never been to this neighborhood before. I fell in love with it instantly."

As we wander down a cherry-blossom-lined canal, I can see why. There's a calm energy here that's a counterpoint to Shibuya. Tiny restaurants without English menus run the length of the canal, and little old ladies carry shopping bags with groceries, while young parents push strollers.

"It's a little escape from all the noise. Don't get me wrong. I love the sounds and lights of the city," she says as we walk to the edge of the canal, stopping at the railing. "But I love finding these little enclaves too. I used to come here now and then when I wanted to . . . go quiet."

"Did you need that a lot?" I ask, imagining her in this same spot a year ago, by herself, staring at the placid water below.

"Sometimes. My job was a little crazy—late nights, wanting to impress the doctors. Every now and then I needed to recharge, so I came here if I couldn't get away to Kyoto."

That's where her folks retired to, three hours away. "Did you see your parents a lot?"

She nods, her eyes sparkling as they do when she talks about them. "At least once or twice a month. Lunches, dinners, or just days spent shopping and wandering around the city. Sometimes I'd go to Kyoto for the weekend and crash at their place."

"That must have been nice." I'm both happy for her and a little wistful too, wishing I could see mine for a weekend. "What else did you do while you were here in Tokyo?"

"You want me to fill in the last three years?" she asks, with a laugh.

"Kind of."

"Besides missing you?"

I scoff. "You didn't miss me that much."

She stares sharply at me. "Did you miss me?"

"You know I did."

"And I missed you. I thought about you a lot," she says, her words soft and tender, thawing a cold piece of me.

"So we were sad sacks, missing each other," I tease.

"Maybe we were. I mean, look. It was hard, but I had to focus on school and so did you. We agreed to that, and I think we both did that. But I also didn't ever stop thinking about you."

Her admission kick-starts another part of my engine. I reach for a strand of her hair because it's almost impossible to *not* touch her at a time like this. "Did you think about me when you drew blood?" I ask, in a pretend-sexy voice.

She laughs and responds in a smoky tone, "When I gave shots too."

I wiggle my eyebrows as I run my fingers along that strand. "What about when you took temperatures?"

"All the time. Just like I'm sure you couldn't stop thinking of me when you read case law."

"Torts, baby. Images of you got me through torts."

She laughs loudly.

I let go of her hair, and she nudges my waist with

her elbow. "It's good to be here with you. To show you stuff. Want to see the neighborhood?"

"I do."

We spend the rest of the day wandering through this quieter section of the city as she catches me up on nursing school, doctors she worked with last year on the job, friends she made, and days she spent seeing her parents and her sister. I notice she doesn't mention a boyfriend, or any guys for that matter. I can't resist asking, even if it's sticking my finger in the flame. Maybe I need to know if it'll burn. "Did you date? See anyone?"

She shakes her head, and I relax slightly. "Not really, no," she answers.

"Not really or no?"

"C'mon. They're pretty much the same. The point is I didn't really date. I didn't meet anyone I fell for. Did you?" she asks, turning the question back on me as we round a street corner. "Some pretty legal eagle?"

My lips curve into a grin. "Not really. No."

"Not really or no?"

"Holland, I didn't meet anyone I fell for. That would be a logical impossibility."

She lifts her hand and gently runs her fingers over my hair. "Good. I don't like the thought of you falling for someone else."

That's one thing she won't ever have to worry about.

20

Andrew

The next day I meet Kana at the park, and she guides me through streets I never knew existed. I try to swat away a nagging worry that after all this, after five thousand miles, I might leave with no more than I came with. What if there's *nothing* at the teahouse, and all I learn is Ian liked to drink tea? No conclusive evidence. Case closed.

As we dart across a busy intersection, I make myself focus on Kana and what she's saying about Tokyo. We turn onto a quieter road as she chats about how the city was built this way after the wars, with zigzag streets that crisscross haphazardly to make it tough for invaders to march straight through the town and seize it.

"The city itself was designed to protect its citizens," I say.

She nods enthusiastically. "Such a smart strategy, but sometimes it backfires. I've lived here most of my life, and I can't always find everything."

"You seem to be doing a pretty good job," I say as she points to a narrow alley to turn down.

At the end of a street that's more like a narrow stone path, we reach a wrought-iron fence. Kana opens it, and I follow her into a small, fenced-in garden, then down a winding path, past trees and bushes. Behind the largest tree is a small teahouse, perched at the edge of a pond.

When we reach an ancient-looking door with traditional Japanese writing across the front, she whispers with reverence, "This is the Tatsuma Teahouse."

The words from the website echo in my mind —*very healing cure*.

I stare at the teahouse as if secret hatches will open or hidden doors will invite us in. "All right, teahouse, what have you got?"

"There's a legend that the tea leaves are not ordinary tea leaves. That they have mystical powers."

Mystical powers. Is that what Ian believed? Was he going for broke and defying all logic . . . *fighting like hell to live*, no matter what?

"Tell me everything," I say, sounding desperate to know, because I am.

Kana straightens, spreads her arms as if summoning an ancient spirit, and then begins. "There's a legend that one of the Japanese emperors a long time ago had a young and beautiful wife, who had suddenly taken ill. He loved her madly and searched far and wide for the best doctors to treat her. But with each successive doctor, she grew more ill. She was hallucinating, talking to people who didn't exist. But the emperor loved her so, and when she muttered something about the tea leaves in the nearby fields, he went himself to search. And there in the fields near his palace, where only rice had grown before, there was one single row of tea plants sprouting up from the soil."

Kana gestures slowly, gently, as if she's drawing up a tea leaf from the ground. She continues in her hushed tone, and for a second I feel as if I'm in a house of worship.

"He gathered the leaves himself." She demonstrates, as if she's plucking leaf after leaf off a bush. "And he commanded the royal tea master to brew tea with these leaves. He brought the steaming teapot on a tray to his wife, and he poured the cup. She took a sip, then another, and then she looked at him and said"—Kana reaches out her hand as if to place it on a cheek, like she's playing the part of the young wife —"*my love.*"

No wonder Ian was taken with her.

It's in her eyes, her hands, in the way she

recounts her city's folklore. She's enchanting, and in this moment, I see her through *his* eyes: warm, upbeat, outgoing. But also, full of hope and life.

I can see so clearly why Ian was drawn to her.

And to *here*.

This city is perfectly paired with this woman, even if I don't believe in the power of a drink to heal. I'm not a practitioner of legends.

She continues, "Every day she drank more, and every day she grew stronger. And then she was cured."

Cured. Such a gorgeous word, such a painful word. The word I begged for, bargained for, hoped for. The only word in the English language that mattered.

"They were together for many years. They had five healthy children and lived long and prosperous lives. And the wife gave thanks every day for the Tatsuma tea leaves that had grown in the fields when she most needed them."

I want to laugh. I want to scoff. I want to blow this all off. But something about the way she tells the story makes me want to challenge myself—so I can believe in the tea too. It wouldn't kill me to believe in something for once. Ian was the happy one, and lately my heart's been a black hole.

But it's filling in, little by little.

Not every second, not every day. But here and

there—like at the fish market with Holland, like texting with Jeremy, and now.

"Did Ian believe in that story? Because he was the most rational person I knew."

Kana looks into the distance, a tear welling in her eye. She wipes it away. "For a long time, yes. He believed in the possibility with all his heart."

Why didn't he tell me, then? Why didn't he share that story with me?

I knew he was a fighter. And sure, I know he wanted to live. But I was never privy to these deeper hopes.

Maybe he figured I'd never believe them. That I'd laugh. I want to tell him I didn't laugh—I listened.

"Can we go in?" I ask instead.

"Yes," she says and pulls the heavy red door open.

It's like walking into a shrine. The room is lit only by candlelight. Five low tables are arranged on the stone floor, with only cushions as seats, no chairs.

I slip off my flip-flops and place them in a wooden cubby. Kana removes her red Mary Janes. A woman wearing a green kimono emerges from behind a wood door, and they speak in Japanese. She gestures to a table and we sit.

Soon, the woman returns with a steaming teapot and two mugs. She raises the pot several inches in the air and tilts the spout down, filling the cups.

She looks at Kana, and more words rain down. The woman chatters for a minute, then another,

Kana nodding and smiling the whole time. The only words I understand are the last ones that she says to me: "*Domo arigato.*"

"*Domo arigato*," I repeat, wondering what I'm thanking her for.

Kana laughs softly.

"Did I say something wrong?"

She shakes her head. "No. She just said how much you look like Ian."

"That seems to be the theme lately."

"But then she also said she was honored to take care of your brother," Kana says.

"Take care of him?"

"Yes. She served him tea."

"But how is that taking care of him?"

Kana shushes me and urges me to drink.

I take a sip. It tastes like hot barley. What's so special about this *healing tea*?

"How was she taking care of him if he died? There was no cure. The tea wasn't mystical. He's gone. Done. *Sayonara.* The jig is up." My voice is caustic, the words corrosive, because it's hard for me to believe when the evidence says this tea does nothing.

Kana bites her lip, and I watch her throat move, as if she's swallowing roughly, holding in tears.

"Shit. I'm sorry," I say, my head hanging low. "I know you loved him too."

"I did."

"I know it's hard for you," I say. Her eyes are wet, but she's holding strong. Like I should be doing. I breathe in deeply then ask the question others ask of me. "How are you holding up?"

Once I say it, I sit straighter. Asking someone else does something meaningful to me. It changes the score. Makes me feel not so alone at all. This woman I hardly know has more in common with me than I ever expected.

"It is hard," she says, but she manages to smile. "But I try to remember the good times and let them fuel me. Fortunately, Ian and I truly only had good times."

That's why he didn't want her to see him dying. Maybe that was his parting gift to her. The gift of *only* good memories.

It seems to have worked too.

Her smile is infectious. I can't help but grin, because part of me is thinking of the conversation with Holland from the other day. Endorphins, natural painkillers—those are made during good times. I don't really want to be thinking of my brother getting it on, and I'm not—but I also understand. Sometimes, you just need a good woman.

In the worst of times.

In the best of times.

In all the times.

"Tell me about some of your good times with

him." I shake my head and hold up a hand. "Wait. Nothing inappropriate."

She laughs and winks. "Don't worry. I keep those for myself." She dives into story time. "We loved music. We loved a lot of the same music."

I smack my forehead. "Wait. Don't tell me. He won you over with the piano?"

She laughs and shrugs happily. "What can I say? When a man plays John Legend for me, I go all swoony. A man like Ian? I had no choice." She looks away for a second, maybe more, as if she's remembering. "Our first date was at a piano bar. And he did take me to a John Legend concert."

The ticket stub. He went to see the show with her. He must have saved it as a memento.

I learn that my brother was a total romantic. He pulled out all the stops for Kana. He went full repertoire at the piano bar—John Legend, Ed Sheeran, and Matt Nathanson.

"Did he tell you he met Matt Nathanson?" I ask, leaning forward.

"Oh God, he did?" she asks, her pitch rising in excitement.

"That's one of the perks of living in Los Angeles. We run into celebrities sometimes. Once, when we were eating at a café in Santa Monica, he saw the singer and walked right up to him." Kana's eyes widen as I tell the story. "Ian held out a hand and said, 'Thank you. Your music has done so much for me. Well, for my love life, that is.'"

"He said that? That devil," she says, but her smile is radiant.

"Matt Nathanson clapped him on the back and said, 'Happy to help a brother out.'"

"I'll never listen to 'Still' and not think that." The spark in her eyes says the song is another good time. Another good memory.

And I gave her a new piece of it. A new twist on a story. For one of the first times since my brother died, I didn't take from someone—I gave. It feels . . . cathartic, and it feels amazing.

As if another patch in the hole in my heart is filling in.

I lift the cup of tea, and a new piece of understanding slides into place. "Sometimes healing isn't about our bodies," I say, and it feels that way for me right now.

"I believe that's true."

I take another drink. It's not mystical tea. It doesn't bring eyesight to the blind. It doesn't even taste that good. But sipping again makes me turn over a new possibility: maybe what my brother was searching for wasn't healing from the disease, but healing from the way it could hollow your heart.

Maybe Kana was part of that healing. I still don't know what she meant to him entirely. But this much is clear: she was so much more than I thought.

Maybe she was everything to him.

Now that—that I understand.

As I walk home to the apartment that evening, my phone pings with an email.

It's from my sister.

21

Andrew

Laini is going to be in Kyoto in four days. She has business there, meeting with a design studio her film company contracts with. We make lunch plans, and I plan to spend the next few days with Holland. Three days of unstructured time, with hours spilling before us. It feels like the summer we were together, but it also feels entirely new because we go places neither one of us have ever been.

We visit a tranquil fish pond where we give nicknames to many of the fish.

"That orange one? He's Fred," I say.

"The yellow one is Carl."

I point to a blue fish. "She's definitely a Jen."

"Fish should always have standard human names," she agrees.

"But telling them apart remains the challenge."

"Do you think the fish can tell each other apart though?"

I consider this, furrowing my brow as I study the creatures zipping through the placid water. "Probably. I bet Jen says to herself, 'Oh I have a lunch appointment with Carl at noon. We're going to eat some . . .'" I trail off, trying to remember if fish eat plants, algae, or something else.

Her eyes glint playfully. "Smaller fish. They're cannibals."

"I believe that makes them carnivores."

"Tomorrow, let's be herbivores. I have an idea for a lunch place."

The next day we try to find a ramen shop that's been lauded on food blogs, but we wind up so twisted and turned around we figure it was never meant to be. Especially since we stumble across a lunch spot that serves ice-cream-stuffed bread.

I point to my empty plate. "Now this was meant to be."

"This is last meal–worthy."

As I settle the check, my phone rings. I grab it to hit ignore, since I don't want to be rude and answer it in a quiet restaurant, but it's the doctor's office.

I mouth *Dr. Takahashi* to Holland, and she shoos me out.

"Hello?" My voice doesn't sound like my own.

I expect the receptionist, but it's the man himself. "Good afternoon. This is Dr. Takahashi."

I straighten my spine when I hear the deep timbre of his voice. "Good afternoon, sir." He's definitely a sir.

My pulse is rocketing, and I'm all raw nerves as he says things like *doctor-patient confidentiality* and *I don't typically do this.*

Then the next words come, and they're beautiful. "But I understand this is important, and for you I can step outside the bounds. I return at the end of next week. Can you meet me the next Monday at one? The first Monday in July."

"Thank you, Doctor. Thank you so much," I say, and I'm overjoyed that he's bending for me. "I'll see you then."

The *why*—the very thing I came for. He's the star witness in the case I'm trying to crack, and I hope he can finally tell me the answer to clue number three.

When Holland leaves the restaurant, she looks at me expectantly.

I hold my arms out wide, smiling. "I've been granted an audience a week from Monday with the good doctor."

She squeals and claps then throws her arms around me.

I don't know that this is hug-worthy, but for the chance to get a little closer, I'll deem it so.

* * *

At night, we go our separate ways.

That's always hard. Watching her fade into the crowd. I want to reach out and yank her back to me.

But I'm starting to understand she's not leaving each night—she's waiting for me.

Maybe she's waiting for me to see my sister. The doctor. Or maybe to find all the answers.

It's possible she's waiting for something of her own.

Perhaps these days together—from the first day at the market, to the next along the canal, to the fish-pond and ramen adventures—are part of what she needs too.

Whatever it is she's waiting for, I love her more for it.

Don't get me wrong—if she invited me up to her place, I'd be there in a nanosecond or less.

But she doesn't invite me to stay the night.

I don't invite her either. I also don't take any more painkillers. I find I'm not craving them as much.

Maybe that's because I know I'll see her in the morning.

* * *

The next day we visit a clone factory that makes life-size dolls of yourself. "For only seventeen hundred and fifty dollars, you too can make a three-D version of your head perched atop a veritable android body," I say, as we try not to crack up or freak out while surveying the replicas.

"I feel like that's a little, how shall we say, self-indulgent?"

That afternoon, we take the subway to Ginza to check out the capsule apartments.

"Could you do it? Live in one of those?" Holland points to one of the hundred or so box-like rooms protruding from a tower, like Tetris blocks haphazardly arranged.

"You mean if we were in a post-apocalyptic society and that was the only option?"

She laughs. "Sure. Or if you were relocated to the moon, like in that sci-fi book, and you had to live in a prison-cell-sized room."

"I suppose if I had to, I would. But generally, I try to avoid situations where I need to live in a capsule," I say, as we turn away from the odd building. "I kind of like space, and sun, and beaches."

I like, too, that we've fallen into this rhythm—checking out the city together as if we're on a vacation. It sure seems like one. Her new job hasn't started yet, and I'm taking time off. I called Don Jansen yesterday. He was kind, but quick—*"All is well,"* he'd told me. Of course all is well.

She scoffs. "If you like space, you're in the wrong city."

Am I? In the wrong city? Maybe I'm merely playing pretend with her, experiencing a slice of life for a few days, or weeks, before we have to say goodbye again.

I know there's an end date. But now I *feel* it, even more powerfully than I did a few days ago. I want to ask what happens when I return to California, but I don't want to crush whatever this tender new thing is between us. Nor do I want to ignore what seems to be building.

I choose an easier way into the topic of *us*. "It's been fun—these last few days," I say as we pass a shoe store selling high-top Converse shoes decorated with superheroes.

"It has been. It's funny because I thought it would feel all mission, mission, mission. But it doesn't."

"What does it feel like?" I ask, a little nervous, a little hopeful.

She stops and shrugs. "I don't know how to label it."

That's the problem. We're living between countries, between jobs. I desperately want to define us, but maybe what we are is in-between—straddling the past and the present, being in love and being friends, wanting and resisting.

It's not easy for me to accept. I like black-and-white. But you have to play the hand you're dealt.

If my brother had to learn to live between sickness and health, I ought to learn to embrace this time for what it is—*time*.

I don't know where Holland and I are going, or if we're going anywhere, but maybe that's the point.

To not *know*, and to keep stepping forward anyway.

And to enjoy the good times, like fish ponds, ice-cream-stuffed bread, and checking out capsule apartments. These random moments remind me why we fell for each other in the first place. We can talk about anything—what is in front of us, what is next, all the what-ifs.

During the summer we were together, we went to the Santa Monica Pier one evening. She stared with horror at the Ferris wheel, and I asked if she was afraid of heights.

"No, I'm afraid of Ferris wheels. They're terrifying. Let's do the roller-coaster instead."

We sped around the bends and steel curves, screaming into the night. Once we were off that ride, I asked what else she was afraid of.

She'd tapped her lip and hummed. "I'm definitely afraid of getting locked in a gas station bathroom. Also, clowns."

I shuddered. "It's impossible to be unafraid of clowns."

"There's one more thing," she'd added, looking at me.

"What is it?"

She took her time before she spoke, meeting my gaze. "Being far away from you," she said, then grabbed my shirt collar. "I'm going to miss you so much."

It wasn't the first time one of us had acknowledged *the thing*. The inevitable end of the summer. The inevitable end of us.

I cupped her cheeks. "I'm going to miss you so much too."

We'd tried to figure out a path through the next three years. We'd played our options like moves on a chess board. What if we flew back and forth? What if I tried to go to law school in Tokyo? What if she tried to get loans instead of accepting her full ride?

What if, what if, what if . . .

In the end, time and distance won the battle, vanquishing our hopes and dreams.

Those two forces will likely checkmate us again. We won't be *in-between* once I board a plane and slingshot myself back to the United States. We'll be apart.

And I'll miss her so fucking much.

Probably more.

That's why I don't want to waste a chance at *good times* now.

"Will you come with me to Kyoto tomorrow?"

She smiles. "I was hoping you'd ask."

22

Andrew

I wait at the train station in the morning, looking around for Holland. I don't see her among the sea of people moving like schools of fish toward train tracks, kiosks, and escalators. I turn in circles, scanning for her.

I startle when a pair of hands covers my eyes. But I smile as soon as I smell lemon-sugar lotion. "I can smell you."

"Do I smell good or bad?" she whispers in my ear.
"Neither."

She drops her hands from my eyes, and I turn around to meet her quizzical gaze. "Neither?" she asks.

I wiggle my eyebrows. "You smell the best."

A flash of pink spreads on her cheeks. "Thank you. You smell pretty yummy yourself," she says, then shifts gears immediately. "Are you ready?"

"Ready or not. Also, were you trying to surprise me or trick me?"

She shrugs as we head to the platform. "Neither. I was just being silly."

"Silly or flirty?"

"Do you think I'm a flirt?"

I raise an eyebrow. "Do you think you aren't?"

She laughs. "You're a flirt."

"Yeah, but you started it."

She smiles and looks down the tracks. The silver train coasts into the station. "Maybe I am a flirt. Do you think old habits die hard?"

"I don't see how either one of us can stand before a court of law and deny that."

On the train, we grab our seats, and I take out my phone and my earbuds. "Want to share Pizza for Breakfast?"

"Is that a new band you're listening to?"

"Mike from the food stall sent it to me. Want to listen?"

"I'd love to."

I hand her an earbud, and we lean in close, sharing the music and the headphones as the train pulls out of the station.

Midway through the fifth song, I slide a finger across the screen, angling my phone away from her.

Andrew: Do you like the music?

Her phone buzzes from her pocket and she grabs it, laughing as she reads the message. She taps out a reply.

Holland: Sort of. What else do you have?

Andrew: Tons of tunes. What do you like?

Holland: Surprise me.

I find another band and hit play. Holland makes an *ick* face.

I switch to another one, and she gives a thumbs-down. I try one more, and she pretends to gag.

Andrew: You're tough to please.

Holland: Not in the least. You always know how to please me.

I cast my gaze to her and mouth, *Such a flirt*.

She mouths back, *Same to you*.

I scroll through my playlists. It hits me—like a flash of lightning across a darkened sky. Feeling a little bit like a movie-star hero who uncovered a secret weapon, I head to Spotify and find what I'm looking for.

I hit play, and a few seconds later, Matt Nathanson croons in our ears.

The smile that lights up Holland's face is magical. She turns to me and mouths, *I love him*.

I imagine she said *I love you*, and it feels like the most right thing that could happen not just to me, but in the universe. I close my eyes, listen to the refrain, and take a chance. I reach for her hand and take it in mine. Our fingers slide together, and it's electric and comforting at the same damn time.

When her fingers curl around mine, I breathe out, a wonderful exhale. I smile like a fool too. My eyes are closed, my music playing, and my girl's hand is in mine.

It doesn't matter that she's not mine yet. It doesn't matter that we're in-between. Right now, we're on the same page. I can feel the connection in the same way I can feel this music humming in my body.

I imagine everyone on this train has disappeared and it's just Holland and me. We ride the train as far as it goes, into the night, an endless night together. It could spill into the next morning, then the next one, then the next.

This connection is more than chemistry and stronger than history. It's fueled by the present and stoked by a raw sort of knowingness—she knows me inside and out, no games, and no pretending.

I know her in the same way.

I know something else that's starkly true. I can't let go of the piece of my wasted, ragged, worn-out heart she irretrievably owns.

It's a permanent piece of my real estate that she has all the property rights to, for perpetuity.

The train slows at our destination a few hours later, letting us out at Kyoto Station, a sleek, metal, modern spaceship. Soon we're escaping the crowds and the streets jam-packed with tourists who snap photos.

Holland tells me where to go, kisses my cheek, and says she'll see me when I'm done with Laini. She bounces on the toes of her pink Converse sneakers. "I'm going to have lunch with my parents."

"Tell them I said hi."

"I will."

I watch her go, and it's weird she's doing something as normal as having lunch with her parents, who live three hours away from her here in Kyoto. But it doesn't hurt thinking of her plans, and it doesn't hurt watching her head to see them.

It's just her normal, and this is mine: meeting my sister.

I find my way through the quieter alleys, the small shops, and the narrow lanes that lead in and out of gardens and temples, and that bring me to a walking path that runs along a stream. A narrow set of steps looms in front of me. After five minutes of going vertical, the steps end at a stone bench that looks out over the gurgling water below.

Laini sits on the bench. She stands, and for a second, I think she's going to simply wave, but instead, she closes the distance and hugs me hard.

"It's so good to see you."

When we let go, she's crying.

I don't think I've ever seen my sister shed a tear.

23

Andrew

Since Laini is fifteen years older than I am, it'd be easy to think I'm the "oops" baby. But there's the pesky case of the middle child, eleven years younger than her.

Since our parents had Laini when they were in their early twenties, Ian and I decided she was the "oops" baby. But by the time we got around to knowing what an "oops" baby was, and teasing her about it, she was long gone.

That's the thing about a big age difference—Laini is more like an aunt than a sister. She wasn't a big part of my life growing up. I don't remember when she lived with Mom, Dad, Ian, and me since she left home when I was three and Ian was seven.

She wasn't a part of our lives. We weren't a part of hers.

When our parents died seven years ago, Laini was already married, with one child and another on the way. She returned for Ian's memorial service in May and was gone just as quickly, back home to India.

I hardly know her, and I hardly know why she's in tears. "What's wrong?"

She doesn't answer. Only sobs harder.

Fear runs through me. "Are you okay? Are you sick?"

"I'm fine," she says, all wobbly. "It's just so good to see you."

I furrow my brow. What the hell is going on with my sister? She's never been affectionate, but as she leaks tears, she tightens her hold on me.

"It's okay," I say gently, patting her hair, since I think that's what I'm supposed to do. I've never been the one to comfort, and the only female I've been close enough to help—Holland—was always the strong one.

More tears fall, and I keep murmuring, "It's okay. It's okay. It's okay."

Laini loosens her vise grip on me, fixes on a smile, and swipes at her cheeks. "There. That's done. I'm all good now."

I laugh incredulously. "You just needed a good cry?"

"I think I did."

I shake my head, trying to make sense of her. "Who are you?"

She squares her shoulders and adjusts the strands of brown hair that have fallen from her loose bun. "I'm Laini, and I'm the bad sister."

"Don't say that," I say softly.

She smiles ruefully. "I am, and I know it, and I'm so glad you reached out. I brought lunch. You were always a big eater."

"When I was three?"

She nods. "You could put away a pizza pie then."

"Ah, so that's where my love of pizza comes from —a childhood spent adoring it."

"I hope you like sushi as much."

"Maybe more," I whisper conspiratorially.

We sit on the bench. Laini hands me takeout sushi in a plastic container. I pop a piece of hamachi into my mouth, and as I chew, Laini cuts to the chase. "You wanted to know about the time I saw Ian, right?"

"I do." I take a beat before I say more since I didn't expect her to be so blunt. But if that's the style du jour, I'll continue in the same vein. "It surprised me, Laini. You kind of fell off the map after Mom and Dad died."

She takes off her glasses and rubs the bridge of her nose, nodding. "It wasn't my finest moment. Or moments. But I didn't realize it at the time. I was so caught up in my life, and my job, and being a mom. It was hard for me to process everything that had happened. And I was so far away. I think in the back of my mind that's how I justified it."

"I guess I can see how that would happen."

"But then my daughter turned thirteen several months ago," she says, and holds up her hands like claws then hisses.

I laugh. "Rough times?"

"She's like a whole other person." Laini reaches for a piece of yellowtail and chews. "But it has made me more aware of everything I say to her, of every single word. And how important every word can be." She locks eyes with mine. "That's why I reached out to Ian. To make peace." Her voice is soft, contrite even. The tone of it hooks into me.

"But you weren't fighting with him."

"I know, but I wanted to do more than *not* fight. I wanted to make sure I had a chance to tell him I loved him."

"Was he surprised when you came to see him?"

She shifts her shoulders back and forth, like a seesaw. "Yes and no. Mostly I think he was happy. We talked about my work and my kids, and we also talked about the past. How we felt like we never knew each other as well as we could have, and we missed that. And then I told him I loved him." She raises her hand to tuck a loose strand of hair behind her ear. "I needed him to know that."

I picture the tuxedo cat card in Ian's pile of mementos, and the words on it—*so glad we did that*. "He knew that, Laini. He was glad you visited. He kept the card you sent him after."

Her lips quiver. "Yeah? He did?"

I nod. "He kept it with some other important mementos I found when I arrived. Didn't take a lawyer to assemble the clues," I say with a smile. "He was absolutely glad."

She lets out a breath. It sounds like it's one of relief.

I feel a momentary peace thinking about how Laini was finally able to say the important stuff to Ian before he died. That's a gift, in a way, to be able to have the last thing you say to someone be the last thing you want them to have heard from you.

Ian didn't need to tell me they had met up. He had found his peace. He had restored another relationship important to him.

He had said goodbye.

I shift the conversation to her kids, learning her daughter is taking guitar lessons and her six-year-old son loves to make his own comic books. Her husband works hard, but plays hard too—he's taken up badminton for fun since he's mastered cricket.

"And how are you doing?" she asks. "I send you emails every week, but you don't say much."

"It's hard for me to say much. To anyone."

"But how are you?" she asks again, pressing.

A bird chirps in a nearby tree as I consider her question. A few weeks ago, my answer would have been empty and numb. Even a few days ago, I'd have said raw and exposed. But none of those are the adjectives I'd choose today.

"I'm better," I say.

I'm stretching and reaching. I'm grasping for something I can almost touch with the tips of my fingers.

Possibilities.

I don't think Laini and I are going to be best of friends. I doubt we'll be the brother and sister who catch up each week over long, friendly phone calls. I suspect we'll always be merely an item on the other's email to-do list.

But she's still my sister, still my family. I drape an arm over her shoulder. "Hey, Laini."

"Hey, Andrew."

"I love you."

"I love you too."

Sometimes that's enough of a reason to see someone. Most of the time, it's the only reason that matters.

24

Holland

The clean, antiseptic scent excites me.

The feel of scrubs sends a little thrill through me.

And the prospect of taking temperatures, checking pulses, and helping those who need it turns me on.

Not in a sexual way.

In a professional way.

As I hand in the final set of paperwork to the head nurse a few days later, I can't rein in the smile. I start my new job in a week, and I can hardly wait.

Harumi Ikeda looks up from her desk. "Thank you very much, Nurse St. James," she says in Japanese.

I bow my head. "Thank you very much, Nurse Ikeda."

She runs her finger over the paperwork, nodding as she checks the photocopies of my work documents.

When she's finished, she raises her wrinkled and weather-worn face, her eyes tired behind her glasses. But she smiles too. "We are so glad to have you here. We hope you will be with us for a long time."

Since the medical center sits in the business district, it attracts expats as well as English speakers on longer work assignments. My fluency in both languages is one of the reasons I snagged this plum job, a rare opportunity for someone who only has a year of experience.

"I hope I will be here for a long time too."

After I finish, I leave the medical center and text my mom as I head to the street.

Holland: Loved seeing you and Dad the other day. Hopefully, we can do that again soon!

Mom: We want regular lunches. Maybe dinners too? London will be coming through Tokyo next month, so we must plan a fancy sushi dinner in early July.

Warmth rushes over me, and it has nothing to do with the late June weather and everything to do with how fantastic that night sounds. It sounds so great that I want Andrew to join us, like he used to when we were younger, hanging out with my parents and my sister. I'll have to ask him if he can join us.

Holland: Activating plans for fancy sushi dinner with the family. ☺

When I tuck my phone away and drop my shades over my eyes, the smiley-face feeling vanishes. Reality sinks in as I make my way through the midday business crowds.

I can't believe I let my mind trick me into thinking I could simply invite him when I don't know if he'll be here or how long he'll stay.

He can't stay forever.

He probably can't even stay much longer—he has a home, a business, and a dog in Los Angeles.

I have a great job and a family *here*.

History is repeating itself. The ending looms, but yet the time with him feels worth the inevitable end.

These last several days with him have been intense, wonderful, and hopeful. As I weave through the crowds, I replay my moments and nights with Andrew, starting with Ian's death, when his life changed irrevocably.

Like a flip book, I see him in anguish, then stuck in a cruel sort of emptiness, spinning his wheels. But the images slowly shift, as if he shucked off the heavy cloak of grief when we stepped onto the plane.

Over here, I've seen him smile and laugh, tease and play. He's become not only the man he was before, but a new man. He's stronger and tougher, but kinder too. I see it in his eyes, in the little gestures, in how he talks to me, and how he talks to others. I notice it in his willingness to seek, his courage to find, and in how he's enjoying the little things again—naming fish, debating capsule life, and flirting on trains.

Flirting off trains.

Flirting everywhere.

I can *feel* the changes in him—in his kisses. The way he kissed me by the vending machine last week made my heart spin round and round, and it tasted like candy and music rather than pain and sorrow.

I picture a whole new flip book—him coming to dinner with my parents, cooking noodles with me after work, and waking up tangled together on a lazy Sunday morning. We'd skip breakfast and have each other instead.

There's so much I want to do with him: go to the

movies, the arcade, baseball games, and karaoke. Then I want to bring him to my place, dim the lights, and let him kiss me madly, everywhere, the way only he can.

Yanking out my phone once more, I start a text to London.

Holland: You'd be proud of me. I haven't rescued him. He's saving himself.

But I don't hit send. Because it sounds like I'm trying to prove something. I don't need to prove Andrew to anyone. I know, deep in my heart and mind, he's healing.

And it's not because of me. I've been by his side, but I've given him the space he needs. He's making huge strides, but I've made the little ones I needed to make too. I haven't taken on all his burdens. He's bearing them, and watching his heart heal piece by piece makes me fall harder and faster for the man he is today.

I don't want to miss another chance in the present. I'll take what I can get—some of him now, if he'll have me. I'll risk another heartbreak because he's worth it.

I open his contact on my phone.

Holland: Hey, handsome. Want to go to the karaoke bar tonight?

25

Andrew

Something is in the air tonight.

And it's not only the Phil Collins song that I sing.

It's the clothes Holland is wearing.

Usually, she likes jeans and short skirts. Tank tops and bright tees. She's always been casual California girl.

Tonight though? She's decked out in an emerald-green dress, with one of those swirly skirts that makes me want to take her out on a dance floor and twirl her around.

Except we're not at a club.

And I suck at dancing.

But I'm incredibly adept at reading lyrics on a screen and staring at the most beautiful woman I've ever known. I do that when the Phil Collins song ends and again when Sam Smith begins, then it's her turn again.

She shimmies her hips as she belts out a Katy Perry tune, crooning about fireworks as that little green dress swishes around her thighs.

Those soft thighs . . .

I know how they feel under my hands.

I know how they feel beneath my lips.

My skin sizzles as I picture kissing her legs.

When Holland finishes, someone else takes the mic, a couple of Japanese girls who tackle Arcade Fire and Adele.

A couple of hipsters wanders in, decked out in plaid pants and bowler hats. They join our patch-work crew, belting Journey's "Don't Stop Believing," then switching to a Bruno Mars number.

We don't exchange names, but we become a temporary karaoke crew. We laugh and toast and hold our vodka tonic glasses high and say *kampai* for *cheers* then sing more songs.

At some point, it becomes guys versus girls, and I'm not entirely sure who's keeping score or how, but someone is, and the women are winning.

Holland takes to the stage to blast out a fantastic "We Are Young" from Fun, and when it ends, they shout at her to "Do Ed!"

She thrusts her arms in the air. "The one and

only Ed Sheeran," she says, smiling so wide it reaches the sky, I swear.

I hoot and holler, because I've no problem rooting for the competition when the competition is her. But midway through "Photograph," my cheers die down as she locks eyes with me. The moment slows, and everyone else fades to black.

Jesus Christ, I'm a lovesick fool, because when she pins me with her gaze, singing about how love can heal and how it can mend your soul, all I see, all I feel is her and me, falling back into each other again.

My heart thumps hard against my chest, wrestling to break free. It squeezes, then kicks wildly, and it's not a new sensation when it comes to her, but it's a different one. It's deeper, more intense, and terribly insistent.

There isn't enough space in this karaoke booth for both me and the way I feel for her. It's too big, too strong.

When she finishes, she purses her lips and blows a kiss my way.

I can't take it anymore. I'm not going to *play* the strong one anymore. I'm going to *be* the strong one. The strong one is going to speak his mind and tell the girl how he feels. No more holding back. I've done that long enough. I'm ready to let go and see where we fall.

I stand, ready to head over to her, grab her hand,

and take her out of here when one of the guys thrusts the mic at me. "You go next."

"Do Rick, do Rick," the other guy shouts, and maybe they mean Rick Springsteen's "Jesse's Girl," but when they punch up the number, I laugh since I'm dead wrong.

It's a good thing you can't mess up Rick Astley's "Never Gonna Give You Up."

As I sing the simple tune, it feels more fitting than I imagined a song that's become an internet prank would be.

It's an anthem to how I feel for this woman. The one who took this journey with me across an ocean. To be my sidekick.

To be my safety net.

I didn't need her to catch me, though, and I'm glad of that.

But I want her desperately. Inexorably. In a way that defies logic and reason but makes all the sense in the world—she gives so much more than I deserve, but she never keeps score.

The cheesy lyrics take on a whole new meaning as I sing to her and only her, letting her know I don't want to give her up or let her go.

When the song ends, I toss the mic to one of the guys. He catches it deftly as I walk to Holland, extend my hand, and tug her up from the couch.

"Come back to me," I whisper.

"I'm already there."

26

Andrew

We don't talk the entire cab ride home, our tightly locked fingers the only communication we need.

She knows.

I know.

I shove the door to my apartment closed.

My lips slant to hers, and I kiss her like the whole night hangs in the balance.

Her hands race up my chest, and we kiss, and we kiss, and we kiss.

I twine my hands in her hair, pulling her blonde waves away from her face. She tilts her head a bit, my cue to kiss her neck, then the hollow of her throat, then behind her ear in a way that makes her gasp. She says my name in a low and husky voice.

The time for slow and tender vanishes, and she doesn't seem to mind. We kiss harder, deeper. She melts into my touch and angles her body closer and closer still.

I can't get enough.

My mind blurs, and my skin crackles, and everything feels different now than it did the last few times we kissed—at the vending machines and at my house in Los Angeles.

Everything feels possible.

Everything feels right.

I break the kiss, my breath coming hard and fast. I can't hold back anymore. I need her to know. I have to say it. "There's no point pretending. I love you so much."

"I didn't think we were pretending." She grabs my face, holds my cheeks. "I love you so much too."

The night sky bursts open. All the stars shine on us. Somewhere, a new rock anthem is born, and it's epic.

I drop my forehead to hers, inhaling the sweet smell of her. "I feel like I'm falling in love with you all over again, but I also never stopped loving you. Does that make any sense at all?"

She laughs lightly and drags her hands through my hair. "It makes all the sense in the world. I'm in love with you in a whole new way now."

My lips curve up into a grin. "Yeah?"

"I don't think you can be undone."

I raise a brow in question.

She taps her chest. "You did something to me long ago, and you're here. Permanently. All these feelings for you—they were latent for the last few years. But now they're back, and they're brand-new, and they're not going anywhere."

My heart soars to another galaxy. This is too much. Too perfect. And for tonight, I want only the perfection of this moment. I clasp her face. "I want you back. I need you back. Be with me."

"I'm yours," she says, with a vulnerable, desperate look in her eyes that matches everything I feel for her. This is letting someone in. This is opening your whole heart.

I scoop her up, carrying her to the futon in my bedroom.

I feel like I've had too much caffeine, or like it's my birthday and all I want to do is open my presents. I tell myself to slow down, to not rip off her clothes, to take my time because we have time. But I don't listen to those plans.

Frantic and frenzied, we undo zippers and tug at buttons, and soon I'm down to black boxer briefs and she's in red panties with white polka dots.

My throat goes dry as I pull them off and gaze at her naked body once more. She's the most beautiful sight. I run a hand along the back of her leg, thrilled to touch her like this. Her body moves against my palm, and she gasps, a soft, lingering sigh. It's all so achingly familiar and so incredibly new at the same time.

She arches into my touch, and my pulse spikes.

I *know* her. I know what to give her.

She lets out the sexiest groan as I run my fingers down her bare legs. "You know I'm not stopping this time, right?"

"You better not."

"Now that we're in agreement . . ."

I start at her ankle, and she shivers under my touch. I look up at her, and she looks down at me, and we lock eyes for a moment. Then she whispers, "Don't stop," and I reacquaint myself with her knees and her thighs, her belly and her hips, and everything between.

I close my eyes as I kiss her where she wants me. She's soft and wet and better than anything.

Her legs fall open, and she murmurs something I can't make out. She's already slipping into the zone, and that's where my girl likes to be. Holland is the most giving person I've ever known, but in bed she's greedy, and I couldn't be happier that she wants pleasure, she wants touch, she wants to be adored.

I can do that. I can give that to her, and I do, going down on her like it's been three years and I'm starving, because it fucking has and I fucking am. I'm so damn hungry for her, and she tastes like heaven on my tongue, my lips, my chin.

I want to be covered in her, and the way she

responds, arching and writhing and chanting my name, tells me she wants all the same things—more and more.

She cries out in bliss, then moans and groans, and the wild noises nearly break my resolve to do it again, since I'm dying to be inside her. But I'm up to the task of giving her another orgasm before I lose myself in her warmth.

I take it slower, kissing the inside of her thighs, nipping her flesh till she's reduced to a twisting, moaning, hot, wet mess that I love. Her hands curl around my head again, wrapping in my hair, and she pulls and tugs and shouts incoherent sounds that are the best serenade ever. It's a perfect dirty karaoke encore as I bring her to the edge once more.

When her gasps slow, I crawl up her body, and she looks drunk on me, smiling like a happy fool, her eyes all hazy, her hair a mess.

Her blue eyes twinkle, and she rises, tugging at my waistband. "Get naked too," she tells me and pushes off my boxers. She groans as she runs a hand along my length, and this—this is better than anything.

Coming back together.

"Hold on."

I reach for a condom from the nightstand. "I was kind of hoping this would happen, so I wanted to be prepared."

She arches a brow. "Kind of hoping?"

"More like fervently wishing and praying."
I wink.

"Ditto."

I unwrap it and cover myself. She curls her hands over my shoulders, tugs me close, and whispers my name.

"*Andrew.*"

She doesn't say "make love to me." She doesn't have to. She knows that's all I've ever done to her. That when I fuck her it's always with love.

It's never been just sex between us. It never will be. When you're inside the woman who makes the hole in your heart disappear, it can't be only physical. It's everything.

She parts her legs for me, and when I sink into her, my world turns neon. I'm high-definition and electric, lit up like this city at night.

As we move, my mind goes hazy, my skin grows hot. Pleasure rushes up and down my spine, racing through every cell in my body.

I want to say something. I want to tell her something, anything—words of love, words of sex. But the power of language has been drained from me, and I'm one giant electrical line, humming, buzzing.

I brace myself on my palms, swiveling my hips, and her eyes lock with mine. An obliterating wave of lust crashes into me as her lips part. She throws her head back and cries out my name again.

I'm so fucking happy I can give her this. It hardly seems equal when she's given me so much more. It probably never will be even, but here in the bedroom, she can take all she wants. I'll gladly give her all the pleasure I can, and I do as she comes again.

It's beautiful and epic the way her orgasm moves through her, and it rattles mine loose—a burst of pure ecstasy that blots out the world.

Right now, *she's* my world. It's the real world times a thousand. It's thunder and lightning and stars.

When I come down from that high, I roll off her, toss the condom in the trash, and bring her into my arms.

Her cheeks are flushed, and she has a happy, woozy look on her face that I want to keep putting there, every night and every day.

"Hi," she whispers.

"Hi."

"I missed that so much I'm not sure how I survived the last three years."

I swallow hard and then decide it's now or never. I prop myself up on my elbow. "Whatever it takes, I want to be with you."

She smiles and traces my jaw with her finger. "I want that too. But what does that mean? Because I'm staying here, and at some point, you're going back. What happens then?"

I laugh and shrug. "I don't know. But I don't want a fucking ocean between us."

She nods sagely. "Oceans can be problematic. Can we find a way to remove it? Tug Los Angeles closer to Tokyo?"

I laugh and pull her close, kissing her forehead. "Shut up. I mean it."

She presses her hands to my chest, pulling back. "I mean it too."

"You want me to move the ocean for you?"

"I mean, I don't want an ocean to come between us." She winces. "But I also have to pee. Can you hold the thought?"

I salute her as she gets out of bed and heads to the bathroom. A minute later, I hear her flush then wash her hands. When the water stops, she opens the door and tilts her head, looking down the hallway at me.

She's naked and curious. But concerned too. "Why are Ian's painkillers open and on the counter in your bathroom?"

27

Holland

I'm fast at counting pills. The label says twenty, and three are missing.

While it's possible Ian took three, there's that little matter of the reason Andrew traveled to this city in the first place.

Unopened meds. *Unused* meds. He showed me the original letter from Kana. It listed all the meds, including Percocet next to the word *unopened*.

There has to be an explanation.

I look straight at Andrew, waiting for his answer. Tension spreads across my shoulders, but the tightness originates in my heart.

His jaw goes slack, and the admission is in his

eyes. He squeezes them shut. "I took some." His voice is ash.

It's only three pills. It's not a big deal. Three pills does not an addiction make.

Heck, three pills are what someone swallows over a few days when he has a bad back and it acts up unexpectedly.

But Andrew doesn't have a bad back.

He doesn't have headaches.

He didn't have surgery, and he doesn't suffer from recurring pain.

He's healthy as a proverbial horse. He has no need for opioids.

"When did you take them?" I try to keep my tone as calm as possible. I don't want to accuse him of anything. I want to know why he's been turning to this drug, even a few times.

"The first night. I was jet-lagged and . . ." His sentence falls off a cliff.

"You took them to get to sleep?" That's not ideal, but if he struggled with insomnia at the start of the trip, I can understand wanting something as a lullaby for the brain.

He rakes a hand through his hair. His voice is clogged with emotion as he answers, "No. It was the time I saw your pictures."

I inhale sharply, wishing that wasn't the reason. "And you needed the drugs to make it through the night?"

"It was only two," he says defensively.

"What about the third?"

He sighs heavily. "I took it the next morning."

I wince, absorbing this information and dreading asking the next question. "Why did you need them?"

He drags a hand down his face. "It was easier. It was just fucking easier than letting my mind entertain such awful thoughts. But that was practically two weeks ago, and I haven't so much as thought about taking another since."

"That's good. That's great."

"You're acting like I'm an addict."

I raise my hands and shake my head. "I didn't say that. I simply asked what was going on. Because I care. Because I love you. I'm glad it was only three."

I move into the bedroom and sit next to him. We're both still naked, and maybe this is fitting. Maybe naked is how we're supposed to bare the most vulnerable parts of ourselves to each other. "I can live with that. I understand it was hard seeing those photos, and your mind leapt to places it shouldn't have, and you were tempted. You needed help." I take a deep breath. "As long as that's all it was, and it's behind you, then you don't have to explain any more."

I take his hand and squeeze it.

He doesn't squeeze back.

He drops his head in his hands and sighs heavily. "I took more in LA."

My heart craters. "You did?"

"I did. I took a bunch."

"When? What led you to it?" Nerves thread through my questions.

"Right after I hit the car, and also before I saw you at lunch on the pier, and a few other times."

A heavy weight tugs me down, pulls me under the sea, sinking my new image of us. "How many?"

"Does it matter?'

"Yes, the number matters."

"Probably a dozen."

I draw a deep breath.

Fifteen total isn't addiction. Fifteen pills isn't a problem.

But it's the me who had three orgasms saying that. It's not the me who's a nurse. It's not the me who sees the danger to both of us. I promised myself I wouldn't be his safety net. I certainly won't be his drug. That's what scares me the most. Maybe he has acted better around me lately—stronger, happier, healthier—but what if that's because I'm the high?

Love is a drug, and it's stronger than Percocet.

I hate asking the question, but I have to know. "Andrew, am I your Percocet now? Am I what's getting you through the grief?"

"No." He snaps his gaze to me. "Not at all. Never."

I want to believe him, but life was harder for him back home because it was normal, everyday stuff he had to deal with—living in an empty home, seeing his brother's things, attending events without his best friend. Even though he's been seeking answers here, his daily life feels more like a vacation—seeing the sights, indulging in treats, taking day trips.

Aside from that one slip-up with the photos, he hasn't had to face anything terribly hard. What if he still needs assistance to help him through?

That's the big issue. That's why I need to know how he's truly doing.

I take his face in my hands. "You're doing so much better, but I want it to be from natural progression, not from me and not from drugs."

His expression is pained. "It was only twice here. That night and the next morning, so it was practically the same time."

My heart crawls up my throat, pushing up tears. That sounds like a justification. "But that *was* about me. You thought your brother and I—" I cut myself off. I won't give that notion the dignity of words.

"It was once. One time."

"But it was before too."

He grabs my hand. "You have to believe me."

"I do." I sound desperate. I feel desperate. "I believe you with my whole heart. But you were taking them in Los Angeles. I'm so happy you're healing. Nothing could make me happier. Nothing in the world. Not puppies, not sunshine, not a million perfect days." I stop, look at the ceiling, and picture what's still ahead of him. "But you're not done. What happens if you find out something hard?"

"What am I going to find out, Holland?" he asks, and his caustic tone sears me.

"You haven't seen Doctor Takahashi yet. Aren't you trying to figure out why Ian stopped taking his meds? Isn't that why you're here? What if you learn that or something else, something you don't even know, and it devastates you?"

"Are you hiding something from me?"

I wrench away. "No. I'm trying to help you, and don't try to suggest that."

"Are you breaking up with me?"

I sigh heavily. "Stop it. Just stop it."

"Are you?"

I take his hand again. This time he lets me. "It would be impossible for me to break up with you, you ding-dong. Don't you listen to me? I fucking love you. That won't change. But I need to know you can handle things without drugs, and I need to know I'm not your painkiller."

His eyes are etched with pain. "I can't lose you again."

My lip quivers. "You're not losing me. But I am asking you to find all your answers to those questions before we dive into how the hell we're going to make this work." Once more, I take his face in my hands. "Do you understand?"

He nods sadly. "Will you stay the night?"

My heart lurches toward the man I love. The man who's not done healing. "Yes, but in the morning, I have to go, and you need to keep stepping forward."

"I will. But right now, I need to do something."

I raise an eyebrow curiously.

He pulls on underwear and shorts and marches to the bathroom. Grabbing the pills, he dumps them into the bathroom trash can then ties up the small plastic bag from the bin. He holds up the bag like a trophy. "Be right back. "

A few minutes later, he returns. "I tossed them in the trash can on the corner. They're gone. I don't need them."

I can see that he believes what he's saying, and I can see how far he's come. But I'll feel better about *us* when I'm certain I'm not his crutch, and that I am the woman he can't live without simply because he loves me. Not because he *needs* me to keep his demons at bay.

I spend the night curled up in his arms. In the morning, when the sun rises, I leave, saying a silent prayer to the universe that he'll come back to me at the end of his journey.

28

Andrew

Four days.

Four brutal days where June melts into July and a sticky blanket of heat sinks down on the city as the calendar flips. The streets radiate heat, and the sun throws it right back again, like it's casting bolts of fire. June was a temptress, a tantalizing geisha with a come-hither wave and a sway of the hips. July, with this cruel combination of intense heat and Holland's ultimatum, is a wicked stepmother.

Fine, technically Holland didn't give me an ultimatum, but it feels like one.

Get your shit together or else. Prove to me that you can.

Maybe she was right to ask the tough questions.

I'm determined to function without her to prove she's not the one who stitched my heart back together.

I'm the one.

And in true Peterson fighting form, I've crushed it solo-style. The first day after PercocetGate, waking up alone, I snagged a guest pass to a local gym and lifted weights.

Then, I visited that food stall, and Mike and I shot the breeze about music and weather and the latest fish hauls.

The next two days, I buried myself in books, studying for the Bar, heading out only for sushi or noodles, and to wander Shibuya at night, becoming part of the crowds.

Today is Sunday and I venture to the Tatsuma Teahouse, reflecting on my conversation with Kana when we were here. I don't go inside, but I stop at the end of the stone path before the wrought-iron fence. I gaze at the garden, the trees and bushes, and the small, unassuming teahouse at the edge of a pond.

I squint, trying to see it through Ian's eyes, to picture how it looked to him the first time he arrived here.

Such a simple place.

But when I reflect back on Kana's reaction to it, I know this wasn't an ordinary teahouse. I'm not sure it was mystical but it meant something to Ian. Something important. Something vital to his health, or maybe, vital to his healing.

I remember my own words that day. *"Sometimes healing isn't about our bodies."*

Ian wasn't healing in the conventional sense, but in some ways, perhaps he was recovering.

But what did I do when faced with a shitty hand? Did I take the painkillers for my body?

No, I didn't.

I took them for another reason. To numb my life. But now as I stare at this teahouse once more, seeing, really *seeing* Ian here, I don't feel the potency of that reason so much anymore.

I don't hang around for long. I'm not a lingerer.

I take off, heading across the city. My destination is the temple my brother went to, since I recognized it as a well-known one from some of the pictures he took.

When I reach it and head up the steps, I bow my head.

I'm not a temple guy, so the bowing doesn't mean much to me personally, but it seems like that's what you should do when you go inside one.

The silence is eerie. The temple is nearly empty. Only a few people are inside, kneeling on the carpet in front of a small Buddha statue.

Quietly, I wander, inhaling the incense, checking out the candles, trying to imagine what Ian did when he was here. If he sat cross-legged on the red carpet. If he bowed. If he prayed even.

Maybe he became a Buddhist.

Maybe he always was one.

Or maybe he came here for the quiet.

For the contemplation.

Because that's what I'm doing, I realize. Taking the time to think, to reflect, to ask questions.

I'm not sure I have all the answers yet, but I believe I'm coming closer. I leave and walk around the streets, looking at shop windows, checking out ramen menus, perusing sections of the city I haven't visited before.

In the afternoon, when the temperature hits eighty-nine, my California soul cries for mercy, and I retreat to the apartment to worship at the altar of air-conditioning and case law.

Kate worked her magic and rescheduled me for the February Bar exam. I hunker down for an hour or two to study for it, but an idea keeps nagging at me.

Tomorrow is my meeting with the doctor. I researched him when Kana first wrote to me, but it wouldn't hurt to refresh. Like exam prep, you read your notes one more time the day before.

I toggle over to Google and review the basic details.

Dr. Takahashi was educated at Kyoto University, did a residency at Mount Sinai, then studied traditional Chinese medicine, especially herbal treatments for cancer. He's known for bringing a rigorous mix of Western and Eastern medicine to patients—

collaborative cancer treatment, he calls it. I scroll through a journal article he penned on new anticancer drugs and advanced therapies then another one on the roles of nutrition, physical exercise, and emotional health in recovery from the disease. I pause at those words—*emotional health*.

I push away from the table, wander to the window, and stare six flights down to the trash can where I tossed the pills the other night. I don't miss them.

A dart of tension shoots through me as I think about tomorrow.

The last leg of the journey. The last chance to find answers.

I shut down my search and return to studying, but I scratch my neck, then my leg, and stare at the ceiling. The walls start to close in. I can feel the presence of my brother too much, and it's clawing at my chest. Making it hard to breathe. I haven't felt this way, too close to him, since I arrived here, but I also haven't spent this much time in his space. I've had Holland here, or I've been in the city exploring. Now I'm here where he spent so many days and nights, and it's just *too much* right now, especially after the temple and the teahouse.

Taking a deep breath, I stand, walk around, try to figure out what I need. Is this what Holland was worried about? I don't want a pill. I want Holland, but I can't remember a time when I didn't crave her and can't imagine a time when I won't. But to have her, I have to figure this out myself.

I need a way out of this feeling—a healthy way.

I call Jeremy on Skype. Maybe some news about Sandy will ease my mind.

He answers quickly. "It's almost midnight. You're killing me."

"Ha. You're always up late. Did you crack level thirty on *Call of Duty* or something?"

"I wish. Just finished reviewing a term sheet."

"What's going on there? How's work?"

"It's great," he says then tells me about the promotion he nabbed at the venture capital firm where he's a junior associate.

"Congrats, man. That's awesome."

"Yeah, Sandy was super excited. She took me out for a nice IPA to celebrate."

I laugh. "I love how you're anthropomorphizing my dog."

"She's practically *my* dog now. She loves me."

"What's she doing right now?"

He switches to video. "This is the one and only time I will do this."

He turns the phone toward my dog, who's snoozing on the couch, legs up in the air. I smile like a crazy man, my heart jumping when I see my girl. "She looks happy."

"She is. Hold on one second. I need to grab a Diet Coke."

He sets down the phone, giving me a perfect view of his ceiling.

That's a little dull.

But five seconds later, there's a snout filling the screen.

"Hey girl," I whisper.

Sandy tilts her head to the side.

"Do you miss me?"

The other side now.

"I miss you so much." I scratch her chin on the screen. Scratch 'n' Sniff dog.

Her ears perk up.

"I'll see you soon. I can't stand being away from you for long," I tell her.

When Jeremy returns, he's not alone. A pretty brunette is with him.

"Andrew, meet Callie. We've been seeing each other."

She's the girl from the photo. Holy smokes. He did it. Jeremy nabbed a woman with my dog greasing the wheels.

"Nice to meet you, Callie." To Jeremy, I say, "Guess you aren't working late, are you?"

He laughs. "I really was reviewing a term sheet. Now, we're going to review other sheets."

She swats him on the shoulder then drops a kiss on his cheek. That's my cue to go.

I thank my buddy again for taking care of my

dog, say goodbye, then drop the phone on the table and stare at nothing for a second.

That itchy feeling has dissipated. The walls are no longer closing in.

Talking to Sandy always sets me straight.

Moving forward is the key. Everything I've done is a step toward the other side of this pain—seeing Laini, talking to Kana, retracing Ian's steps through the city.

Going to see his doctor tomorrow.

I think about tomorrow, and about Ian, and about answers.

Now, I'm seeing paths I didn't notice on the map before.

I'm seeing a problem I think I can solve.

I stand and pace.

There's a zigzagging pattern of ideas in my head, but the lines don't entirely connect. They feel like threads on a conspiracy board in a movie, and I'm trying desperately to connect the dots.

I blink, and the connections start to tighten. The possibilities turn crisper. I head to the entryway table and tap the stack of cards, letters, and the Dodgers cap.

I pick up the magnet from Silverspinner Lanes and flip it over. This one eludes me. But the others . . .

Ideas fly faster, coalescing into one.

Could it be?

Is that the answer?

I need to get outside and clear my head, no matter how hot it is.

I pace through the streets of broiling Shibuya, past arcades, past shops selling socks with hearts and rainbow stripes, past pachinko parlors where people are winning cat erasers and manga figurines. I wander by cell phone stores and crepe dealers and a nail salon, trying to see them all through Ian's eyes. Like the dog mosaic outside the subway station, and the jumbo screen on the building across the street. I'm trying to see everything here through a new prism. I picture my brother at the temple. I see him at the teahouse. A snapshot of him at the fish market shooting the breeze with Mike flashes before me. I imagine what he was feeling.

The noodle shops, the shopping arcade, the concerts, and the woman.

Most of all, her.

Beads of sweat drip from my forehead. I reach for the bottom of my gray T-shirt and wipe my face with the fabric. When I look up at the time, I see the temperature outside the Bank of Tokyo. It's ninety-one degrees, and it's balls hot, but I don't care.

I've figured it out. I'm pretty sure I know what the doctor is going to tell me.

More than that, I think I'm ready for it at last.

29

Andrew

After the temple and the teahouse, I expected a short Zen master in some traditional Asian garb, maybe in a feng shui-ed garden office.

Instead, the doctor is surprisingly tall and also impeccably dressed in a gray business suit.

He doesn't offer me tea, like I expect. Instead, he gestures to the crystal bowl in front of me, filled with lemon and orange hard candy.

"Please. Have one," he says as he pops a lemon candy into his mouth and takes a seat across from me. "I am a candy connoisseur."

I've never been to a shrink's office, but I suspect it feels like this. Like someone trying to make you feel comfortable when you feel displaced.

"Though, truth be told, it's really an addiction," he adds. "I can't stop myself when it comes to candy."

Is he really talking to me about candy? I take an orange one to be polite and put it in my pocket for later. "How was Tibet?"

"Uplifting. I treat the poor and indigent there who are suffering. They are grateful for the help."

He sucks on the lemon candy, his cheek pouching out as he does.

"What else do you do in Tibet?" I ask, because it is so much easier to say that than, *Can you please tell me something I don't know about my brother, or confirm what I suspect to be true?*

He tells me about his work overseas. I hear maybe every three words because I'm focused on what I wish he'd say instead.

"But I suspect that's not why you are here," he says gently, and I want to thank him for putting me out of my small-talk misery.

"No. That's not why I'm here, Dr. Takahashi. You treated my brother. You sent him to drink tea and see temples. Do *you* believe in that legend, then? The one about the tea, about the emperor and his wife?"

"I believe that sometimes if you believe you are healthy, you are healthy."

"Mind over matter?"

"There is something to it, Andrew. There is something to the energy in the universe, the energy you put out, the energy you take in."

Does he truly believe that? I ball my hands into fists. "And does that work for cancer treatment?"

He leans back in his chair and scrubs a hand over his chin as if weighing his words, easing into it. "If you have someone who wants to heal, sometimes they will respond to the unconventional. Their minds are more open to healing, so their bodies become more willing. I believe medication, while a wonderful thing, has its limits. There is value in the unconventional. And Ian wanted that. He asked for that when he initially came to me when he was in remission, and then when we first saw the signs that the cancer was likely returning. I treated him with conventional cancer medicine to try to stave off the return, but also with Chinese herbs and acupuncture. And yes, I encouraged him to go to the teahouse and to see the temples and to keep his mind and heart open to new ways of healing."

"But in the end, he didn't heal," I say heavily, trying desperately to keep a grip on my emotions.

Takahashi presses his hands together and leans forward in his chair. "Your brother was one of the bravest, most resilient people I've ever known. I'm sure you can recall that he was well more than he was not in the last year?"

I picture breakfasts at the fish market, walks with Sandy, and Dodgers games flickering before me. They mingle with new moments, ones I've only been privy to recently—the dates with Kana, the concerts he took her to, a piano bar somewhere—everything that I imagined yesterday when I walked around the city.

A few weeks ago, I wanted to believe Ian went to the doctor for the possibility of a miracle.

But I'm certain now that's not the case. "He didn't come to you for a miracle, did he?"

The doctor shakes his head, and a sad smile seems to tug at his lips, as if he's pleased that I connected the dots on my own. "He knew time was running out. He knew he was dying, but he wanted to heal in his own way, in the only way that he *could* heal at that point."

And so now I am here. The last question. "And he stopped taking the meds because he wanted to . . .?"

But the last word sticks in my throat. I can't get it out because I know that's not the *why*.

He shakes his head. "No. He didn't *want* to die. But he was at peace with it, Andrew. Once the cancer returned earlier this year, that's when he made a choice to finish out his days as free as he could be. He wanted to experience the rest of his life and his death on his own terms."

My throat is clogged with emotions, and my heart hurts, aching with the swell of memories. But I'm almost there. This is what I figured out last night —the truth of Ian's final choices. The *why* is some-thing that I also know I can finally handle. "He came to you first for treatment then for release."

He nods, the sage nod of a wise man. "He asked to be weaned off his meds in a way that was safe." He pauses, bowing his head briefly then meeting my eyes once more. "We spend so much of our time fighting death, as we should. But sometimes the greatest gift we can give ourselves, and in turn the ones we love, is to let go."

It hurts knowing that, but not like I thought it would. Because with knowing comes understanding. It was never about the pills. It was never about tea or treatments.

I stand and hold out my hand to shake Takahashi's. He wasn't Ian's quest for a miracle after all. He wasn't a voodoo doctor in the least.

He was my brother's great hope for a peaceful death, after living a short, but rich and beautiful life.

A life filled with love, with family, with hope.

A last year that unfolded like a dream.

A love he carried in his heart to the other side.

30

Andrew

I'm outside, back on the street I walked down only an hour ago in the Asakusa district of the city.

Asakusa is not Shibuya. It is not neon and lights and flashes. It is subtler—bamboo and temples, kimonos and sandals. It is a long shopping alley with open-fronted stores and carts and people weaving in and out as they hunt for seaweed and fish, for rice crackers and biscuit sticks dipped in chocolate.

I walk along the shopping arcade, part of the flow —the shopkeepers and the workers, the families walking through, and the tourists scooping up folded fans and miniature red cat statues.

Fans.

Statues.

Chocolate-dipped biscuits.

This was where Ian went with the woman he loved.

An older Japanese woman with graying hair and lines around her eyes nods at me as I walk past the Pocky display. I buy some and eat one as I continue on past all this beautiful, wonderful, amazing life.

Toward the very end, Ian was lying on the living room couch under a blanket, petting Sandy, and he said, "Obviously, I'm not going to make it to the All-Star Break this year. But do me a favor? Don't watch the All-Star game. Those games suck."

I'd laughed because it was easier than the alternative.

He rapped his knuckles on my chest. "But if we get back to the World Series, you should go."

I nodded. "I'll do everything I can to get tickets."

His eyes turned serious. "Go, because life is short. Make it count. Don't have any regrets. I don't."

My brother's life was all it could be. He made sure of that.

Because there is no magic cure. There is no secret remedy, no ancient tincture that could have saved him, that could save anyone. The magic is in how he lived, how he died, and the way he loved. Even in his death, he's shown me how to live and how to love.

That's the secret. That's the cure.

I want everything this life has to offer.

I stop for a second and look around at all the

shops and stores and stalls. At all the people going about their days, at all the moments they're living.

This is what I want.

I want to live every moment. I want to feel everything. I want to love one woman.

Together is what I want.

But there's something I still have to do.

The answers have been around me all along—how to live a rich and beautiful life. Ian didn't leave the dossier with the decoder for me, but I found it anyway and the clues turned out to be a true treasure map.

Now I know precisely how to reach the X that marks the spot.

The clues are in the letters, the cards, and the mementos. The path is their meaning. At the end, the words he kept close, and the words he shared, were words of love—the letter from my sister, the note from my parents, the concert stub.

Be a man of actions.

Sometimes words are actions.

I pop into one of the stalls selling paper and buy several sheets and envelopes along with a pen.

I find a table, and I sit and I write.

An hour later, I've said things that need to be said to people who need to hear them. I make some phone calls and make some necessary arrangements. Then I seal up seven different envelopes, head to FedEx, and send them on their way.

One I keep with me.

* * *

Dear Kate,

Sometimes we don't say often enough that we're thankful. I certainly haven't said it often enough to you.

You've helped me in so many ways the last few months, most of all by calling me on my crap. I know it felt like I wasn't ready to hear it. At times, I probably wasn't, but I promise you got through to me. I promise, too, that I'm still grateful for you not giving up. Thank you for all you did.

P.S. Next time you go to Animal House, there will be a gift for you.

Love,
Andrew

* * *

Hey Jeremy,

Are you shocked I'm writing a letter? Me too.

But some things need to be written down, not texted, and not phoned in.

That party you threw for me in June? I was kind of a dick about it. Well, I wasn't kind of a dick. I was a dick. You were trying to help, and I appreciate it, even though I did a shitty job showing it at the time. I'm trying to show it now—thank you.

Also, the fact that you took care of my dog is one of the nicest things anyone has ever done for me. I kid you not. It's buddy movie–worthy.

I wouldn't trust that dog with anyone but you, and I'm so fucking happy that she helped you nab a cool woman.

A few days after you receive this, I'll be sending something to your house. I'll let you know the time. But that, I'll text to you.

Your friend,
Andrew

* * *

Dear Trina,

I'm so sorry I put you in a difficult position. That was

terribly unfair. I begged, and I pleaded, and I did every-thing I could to get you to do something unethical. Thank you for bending for me, and thank you for not bending anymore.

P.S. I have a gift for you. It should arrive in two days.

Love,
Andrew

* * *

Dear Mrs. Callahan,

You might not be expecting to hear from me, but I wanted to thank you for checking in from time to time. Few people do that.

Also, your green thumb is seriously impressive. Thank you for tending to the flowers in the front yard. They look beautiful and the lawn does too.

Best,
Andrew

* * *

Dear Omar,

Your pizza is the best in the world. It helped my brother and me through some really tough times, but you know what? So did all those conversations about the games.

Have I mentioned your pizza is the best in the world? It's so good, in fact, that you can expect a little something extra as a tip next week.

Andrew

* * *

Dear Laini,

I'm glad we got together. Let's do a better job staying in touch. I'd love to see you again soon, and if you're ever up for a visitor in Mumbai, I'll make the trip.

By the way, I love you.
Andrew

* * *

Dear Kana,

Thank you so much for reaching out to me with your letter this summer. I'm not joking when I say it changed my life.

It changed it for the better.

It gave me hope. It gave me focus. It gave me a purpose when I was floundering.

Ultimately, it led me to the answers I most needed to be happy again.

Thank you, especially, for telling me stories about my brother. I'm so glad you came into his life because I now see you were why he was so joyful.

P.S. Do you have any idea what the Silverspinner Lanes magnet was all about? The last time I went with him to that bowling alley was ages ago. He beat me, landing two strikes, if I recall. It was one of his best games, and we had a great time.

Andrew

31

Andrew

I turn down a quiet alley and call Holland. She answers on the second ring, distant, but still kind, when she says, "Hey, how are you?"

"I'm good. I'm great actually. How are you?"

"Fine. Just prepping for my new job."

There's the chatter of crowds in the background. "Where are you right now?"

"I'm over in Harajuku. I'm shopping for a lunch bag, since my job starts tomorrow."

She's so matter-of-fact, and it's so clear she's waiting for me to say something that changes the score.

"Can I see you? I need to talk to you."

She sighs heavily. "You know I want to see you, but why is this different? What changed?"

"I saw the doctor today."

Her tone shifts, softening. "Oh wow. How was it?"

"I didn't need pills to get through it."

"Good. I'm glad." I can hear a faint smile in her voice.

"I want to tell you about it. Tell you what I realized."

"Tell me now."

I nod, taking it on the chin, the directive that she's not ready to see me yet. I can't just wave my magic wand and tell her I'm all good. "You were right. It was hard, but it didn't hurt as much as I thought it would. You were right about other things. I needed to finish, to see this journey through, and I had to do it on my own." I manage a small laugh. "You kind of gave me the ass-kicking I needed."

"And I didn't even have boots on." I hear the smile in her voice widening.

I lean against the wall. "Listen, Holland. I know you were worried I was using you to get through the pain, and I'd be lying if I said you don't make me feel better. Because you do. With you, I feel fucking amazing. But it's because I love you. Because I'm crazy for you. Not because you're a Band-Aid or a panacea." I drag my hand through my hair, more words tumbling out—words that need to be said. "And yeah, there were probably times back in LA when I was desperate to have you with me because you and Sandy were the only ones who made a day better. But that's because I love you two. Madly."

"The dog is very lovable."

"You're very lovable."

She sighs tenderly. "You know I'm stupid in love with you. But I need to know I'm not a crutch. I'm not asking you to never be sad, and I don't want you to feel like you have to fake your emotions about anything when you're with me. But I don't want to jump back in and then learn you're not truly ready." She pauses like she's prepping to say something hard. "Are you? For real now, good times and bad times?"

So damn ready that adrenaline is coursing through me, anticipation winding tight in me. And hope too.

"I'm ready, for good times and bad times. Seeing the doctor, hearing about Ian—it was just that. It was a good time, and a bad time. But I made it through. And after I saw him, the first thing I wanted to do was see you, but I knew I had something else to do first."

"What's that?" She asks curiously.

"I wrote letters to Kate and Omar and Trina and Mrs. Callahan and Jeremy. Kana too. And even my sister."

"You did?" There's a note of sweet surprise in her voice.

"Yeah, like a twelve-stepper. I apologized to some of them for the times I was a dick. And to the others, I thanked them all for the different ways they helped me. They won't get the letters for a few days, but I need them to know they matter to me."

"I'm proud of you," she says in a wobbly voice.

"Why does that make you proud?"

"Because most people don't do that. They don't see the opportunities every day to let the people in our lives know they matter. And you did it."

I tell her more about what the doctor said, and how everything clicked for me the day before. "I knew before I went to see the doctor. I knew when I was finally ready to know. Ian made his choice, and it was driven by what he needed to be happy. The thing is, I'm not sad anymore," I say, and it feels good to voice this. "Well, it's a different kind of sad. A kind I can live with, that's not crushing me. But I feel as if a burden has been lifted. I understand him even better now. He was always the person I was closest to, and losing him devastated me. And at first, I wished he'd shared everything with me, but now I know why he didn't."

"Why?"

"Because he knew I'd have been a selfish shit," I say, laughing.

She laughs too. "You would not."

I nod savagely. "Oh, I would. I absolutely would have begged him to fight, to take anything to live longer. But it was his choice. That's what I see now." I take a breath. "We all have choices. And I made the choice, too, to deal with all this on my own. Without assistance. Without you, Holland. Because you're not my fucking drug. You're the love of my life, and I don't want to spend another second talking to you on the phone when we're in the same city. Can I please see you now?"

This time there's no pause. No tentativeness. No distance. "Come to Harajuku."

"Do you know that vendor who sells potato sticks with sriracha sauce?"

She scoffs. "Do I know it? Or do I worship at the altar of sriracha-covered potato sticks?"

I laugh. "They are indeed worthy of prayers. Can you meet me there in thirty minutes?"

"Yes."

* * *

The longest minutes I've ever spent sludge by as I wait, pacing the platform like a caged animal for the next train. When it appears, I want to reach out, stretch my arms, and yank it closer. Finally, it stops, and the doors slide open. A few stops and a few minutes later, I'm racing up the steps two at a time, and then I run across the street seconds before the traffic light turns red, the cars and cabs a few feet away from me.

I speed through the evening crowds, racing past fashion boutiques blasting pop music and street vendors selling big sunglasses. At the end of the street, waiting by the potato stick vendor, is the woman I love, holding a basket of the savory snack. I see my future, and it's bright and beautiful.

She spots me, and her face lights up. I walk closer, and she does the same, and I'm sure my heart is beating outside my body. I want to hold her tight, to draw her in for a kiss, but there are things that need to be said first.

"Let's go somewhere quieter. We can talk and eat potato sticks."

We make our way out of the busy section of Harajuku and over to nearby Yoyogi Park where we find a bench under a tree, while twilight falls over the city.

I waste no time taking her down memory lane, just like we did the night before our first kiss ever. "Do you remember that time when we were in high school and our parents had a barbecue and we thought we were so cool because we sneaked away to go to the coffee shop?"

"Those were the best lattes I'd ever had."

"How about that time in college when we got together and played Scrabble one weekend during the summer?"

"I beat you with *savvy*—double *V*s and a double-word score, and it was awesome."

"It was especially awesome because you wore this low-cut blue shirt, and I kept trying to sneak a peek."

"Pervert."

"I know, but in my defense, you're crazy-hot, and it was hard not to look at you. It was even harder not to tell you how I felt about you."

"Why didn't you say something?"

"I don't know why. But I don't want it to take years again." I take a breath and place my hand on her thigh. She looks down at my fingers then up into my eyes. "What I realized today is that as long as our hearts are beating, we have choices, and there's one I want to make."

"What is it?" she asks tentatively.

"I told you about the letters I wrote today. To all the people I care about?"

She nods.

"You're one of those people."

Her lips curve up in a smile. "A letter for me?"

I'm not nervous.

Maybe I should be.

But I've been to hell and back, and whatever happens next—whether it's her yes, or her no, or her maybe—I can handle it.

She's the strong one.

But so am I.

That's who I've become, thanks to coming here and meeting all these people, thanks to seeking and to finding.

I take the last letter out of my pocket, unfold it, and hand it to her.

Excitement races through me as she slides her thumb under the flap, opening the envelope. She unfolds the page. Her eyes widen, and she looks down at the note, then me, then the note, then me.

"Are you serious?"

I nod. "I am."

32

Holland

This is a dream.

I'm going to wake any second. It's a fantasy come true. If he means what I think he means, I'm going to squeal so loud they'll hear me in Kyoto.

But just in case I have it wrong, I take a breath, center myself, and do my best to calm down. I hold the paper in shaky fingers. "What do you mean exactly?"

He shoots me a teasing look. "Was it confusing?"

"I want to be crystal clear. Just spell it out for me, please. I want this so badly, but I don't want to get my hopes up for nothing."

He takes my hand and threads his fingers through mine, holding tight. "I want to be with you.

You said we would talk about it and figure things out, but the way I see it is simple—you live here, you have a job here, you have family three hours away. I happen to have more money than most guys my age, on account of inheritances. That's the luck of the draw, and the way I see it, I can either sit on all of that money for a later date, which sounds ridiculously stupid, or I can use some of it to have the life I most want right now—this second. Plus, I do own an apartment here outright, and it's big enough for two. I want to stay, and I want you to move in with me. That's why I wrote this letter."

Dear Holland,

Would you like to be my roommate? I have this place in Shibuya . . .

Love,
Andrew

The waterworks start. Tears break free, and I can't believe he's saying this. I can't believe he'd move here to be with me.

He presses his forehead to mine as he ropes his arms around me. "This is how I can move the ocean."

I can barely speak. I'm overcome with so many emotions, so much joy.

The man I love isn't leaving. He's choosing to stay. He's choosing us. *He's choosing me.*

His lips find mine, and he kisses me. He kisses me like he loves me, like he's in love with me, and like he's staying.

In his kiss, I taste hope and a future.

We pull apart for a second and look at each other, sharing crazy grins. I move in for another kiss, clasping his cheeks as if I'm claiming him. I kiss him hard and deep and with an intensity that is out of this world, or maybe it is clearly *of* this world.

"Is that a yes?" he asks.

"Yes, you can move here. Yes, I want to live with you. Yes, I want to have a life with you every day. But what about your dog and your law firm?"

He holds up a finger and clears his throat. "I have a plan for both."

33

The freeway was clogged, but Kate knew all the back roads to her gym, and she navigated them seamlessly, taking the least-congested route there in less than fifteen minutes. She knew all the ways around a problem. That was what she did in her job in the import-export business—find the quickest way from A to B.

She pulled up to Animal House, planning to attack the boxing bag today before she tackled how to deliver a shipment of rugs to Seoul.

She headed into the gym, nodding to Jimmy at the front desk, then sliding him a check. Animal House was old school—no credit cards for memberships.

Jimmy shook his head. "Your money is no good here."

She gave him a look. She was good at giving looks. "I'm good for it."

Jimmy smiled. "Your membership is paid for the rest of your life. I just got the check from your cousin Andrew."

Kate froze for an unexpected second. Then she clasped her hand over her mouth, pursing her lips.

That boy, he was going to be all right.

"That's a half pepperoni and half cheese pie. You want Caesar salad too?"

The woman on the end of the line said, "Caesar salad sounds delicious."

Omar smiled. "Here at Three Martians, our Caesar salad is the best in town. It comes with my personal guarantee."

He finished the order and hung up, then barked out the instructions to his guys as the bell above the front door rang.

A deliveryman pushed inside, holding a box. "I have a delivery for Omar at Three Martians."

"That's me. Have you got my tomato sauce order in there?"

The deliveryman shrugged. "Doesn't feel that heavy."

Omar took the box, grabbed a knife, and cut a line through the packing tape. When he opened the flap and peered inside, a wide smile spread across his face.

He went to the sink, washed his hands, and returned to the treasure—hundreds upon hundreds of baseball cards. He knew what he was going to be doing that weekend. Sorting through these beauties and enjoying the hell out of them.

* * *

Trina took the last sip of her coffee and reviewed the day ahead of her at the hospital before she left her apartment and headed to her beat-up old Honda.

But the Honda wasn't the only car in her driveway. Next to it was a gleaming red beauty—a sports car she recognized. A huge white bow was tied over the hood, like in TV shows, in the movies.

She'd received Andrew's letter earlier in the week, and it had meant so much to her. This was his handiwork too. When she found a note under the bow, she shrieked.

"Holy crap! I finally have a car that works." She lifted her face to the sky. "I miss you, Ian. And you need to know your brother is awesome."

* * *

That night, stars twinkled somewhere above the haze

of the Los Angeles skyline as Jeremy tickled the ivories.

He'd always been partial to Frank Sinatra, and it turned out Callie liked Ol' Blue Eyes too. He banged out "Fly Me to The Moon" on his newly acquired piano, the one delivered earlier that day. Callie sat next to him, draped an arm around him, and pressed a kiss to his cheek. "You're hot when you play the piano."

He wiggled his eyebrows. He hadn't needed the piano to win the woman. But he liked playing for her, and more so, he liked the thought behind this piano, and what his friend had done for him.

Andrew didn't need to give him this, but Jeremy sure was glad to have it, and he planned to make full use of it.

34

Andrew

They don't call my cousin the fixer for nothing.

Taking care of the car insurance is nothing compared to the rabbit she pulls out of a hat in one week.

In mid-July, my dog arrives by private jet, well-rested and ready to fetch tennis balls. At the airport, I say thank you to Kate's rug-dealing client for letting my dog hitch a ride over the Pacific in such style.

While arranging a shipment of antique rugs to Seoul, she finagled a detour here for my girl. A little extra money made it all possible, and it was money I happily spent.

Kate, ever the wizard, even made some calls so

Sandy wouldn't have to be quarantined. That was money well spent too.

I'm confident Ian would approve of how I spent the funds. But it's not his money I spent. I have my own, and I don't miss a dollar of what made this reunion possible.

"C'mere, girl."

At the bottom of the steps, Sandy tugs hard on the leash. The flight attendant keeps a grip on her, practically sprinting with Sandy the final ten feet to me. My dog slobbers me with dog kisses and happy whines, knocking me on my ass on the tarmac.

I bury my face in her fur. "I missed you too, girl."

She wags her tail at one hundred miles per hour and licks me more. Pretty sure she'll lick my face the whole night if I let her.

That evening, Holland and I take her for her first walk in Tokyo, through Yoyogi Park, and all the sights and sounds make her a little bit nutty. She'll get used to them.

"When do you start class?" Holland asks.

"Friday morning."

"Don't think you're going to get out of grocery shopping by claiming you have to study all the time," she says, playfully.

"I will gladly go grocery shopping with you," I say, tightening my hold on the leash.

"Grocery shopping," she remarks, as if it's the strangest thing.

But it is—it's the strangest thing that's now such a normal thing. We can do the normal things together.

We can wake up together, and cook together, and pay bills together.

Most of all, we can be together.

During the day, she's at the medical center. Soon, I'll be taking language classes so I can improve my Japanese for daily living. I'm still studying for the Bar too.

I have every intention of practicing law. I simply plan to do it here. My brother's firm—*my* firm—practices corporate law, and Don Jansen will continue to ably manage the main offices back in California. But we've decided to open up a branch in Japan. I won't practice Japanese law. I have no knowledge of the Japanese legal system, nor any expectations that I could get up to speed. But I *can* work for American companies within Japan and American companies in the States who need an expert while abroad.

It's a niche, but it's a niche that'll work fine for me to meet my bills.

I have my woman, and I have my girl.

I want to bookmark this moment, capture it for the rest of my days. I know there are no guarantees, not in life and not in love. But I'll take what I can get, I'll take what I can *give*. Another chance.

* * *

Kana: The rest of my band is back in town. Want to stop by the Pink Zebra and see us play? We can grab a tea after.

That sounds like a fantastic way to spend an evening.

I write back with a yes.

Then, as the city does everything but sleep, I strip Holland to nothing, and I kiss her all over. I make her moan, make her writhe, take her to the edge of pleasure. Her hands are everywhere on me—my back, my shoulders, my head.

She tugs my hair harder than she ever has, and I love it. I just fucking love it. When she comes again, I roll to my back and pull her on top of me.

I thread a hand into her hair, bringing her face close to mine. "I want to watch you as you ride me," I whisper.

She shivers, lowering herself onto me. She sighs so greedily, so beautifully. I moan loudly.

She's on birth control now, and it's out of this world to feel all of her against all of me.

She rocks on me, moving up and down, swiveling her hips, taking me deep. She looks like a goddess, all that blonde hair spilling down her back, her skin glowing in the moonlight.

I bring my hand between her legs, intensifying her pleasure. She trembles and groans. Soon, I'm treated to my favorite sight: Holland, falling apart, coming undone, saying my name.

The world becomes a blur of electricity and heat as I join her.

She falls asleep in my arms, naked and sated, her warm body wedged against mine all night long. Soft fur presses to my feet, and my dog lets out a snore in the middle of the night.

Yes, this is everyday living. This is everyday loving.

* * *

We get ready together.

We say goodbye to Sandy together, giving her a peanut-butter-filled Kong that'll keep her happy for the evening.

We hold hands in the elevator.

We talk on the train to Roppongi.

We find the Pink Zebra at the bottom of a hill, at the far end of a slim alley, down a set of steps, underground. There is no flashing sign to guide us, only a faded dark-pink one with the name in curvy letters.

Hand in hand, Holland and I walk inside, and the show begins.

I clap and cheer when Kana comes onstage and blows into the sax, her cheeks like a chipmunk's, as if she's Dizzy Gillespie on his trumpet.

She plays with her eyes wide open, with her body

moving like she's giving life to the instrument. Or maybe its notes are what give her so much life, so much zeal.

She notices us at the end of her solo, and her eyes light up like sparklers set off on the Fourth of July.

When the set ends, and she steals away from the band, she asks if we can head someplace quieter.

"Sure. Are you okay?"

She nods and smiles. "Yes. In your letter, which I loved, you mentioned a magnet. Silverspinner Lanes."

"Right. I figured Ian kept it because of our last game played there."

She shakes her head. "That's not why he kept it."

"It's not?"

When we find a quiet café still open, and Kana sits down, the vulnerable look in her eyes and the way she places her hand on her belly tell me exactly why Silverspinner Lanes isn't about me.

"There's something I'm finally ready to tell you."

35

Andrew

My hands tremble. My head echoes with her last words. The café becomes a strange, surreal place, and as the waiter walks to us, it feels as if he's moving in slow motion. He's coming to take our order, and I'm not sure how people can eat on a night like this, how they can drink.

Questions and more questions zip through my brain, but when I open my mouth to speak, I'm not sure I know how to form words anymore.

"How?" is the only word I get out, and I instantly realize how stupid it sounds. I shake my head. "How far?"

Kana's eyes are nervous, and she fidgets with a

napkin as she quietly says, "Five months. I only started showing a few days ago."

The waiter arrives and interrupts us, asking if we want a drink. Holland quickly takes over, ordering club sodas all around.

When he leaves, Kana thanks her for ordering.

Holland is practically bouncing in the seat. I snap my gaze to her, and a dark thought crosses my mind. Did she know about this? Did she hide this from me? But just as quickly as the thought appears, it's gone.

Holland is the dictionary definition of honest. She wouldn't do that. She's simply excited, and she stretches her hand across the table to squeeze Kana's. "I'm so happy for you."

Like that, I know how I'm supposed to feel. What felt strange and surreal crystallizes. Because I see it in the curve of Kana's lips, and the way she whispers *thank you*, and in the tears that slip down her cheeks. "I didn't say anything when you first came to town because I wanted to be certain. Some people wait until the end of the first trimester, but I wanted to wait for the twenty-week ultrasound—to know the baby is healthy. I had it a couple days ago, and . . ." She stops to wipe a tear, a happy one, when she says, "The baby's perfect."

Holland covers her mouth with her hand. Her voice is full of potholes when she says, "That's the best news. Well, the baby is the best news. I'm so happy for you."

A smile stretches across my face. "So am I, Kana. I'm thrilled," and I mean it.

That's what's so odd. If I take my pulse and my temperature, I'd have to ask if I'm sick. Because the me of a month or two ago wouldn't have responded like this.

I don't know how I'd have taken this—maybe caustically, maybe sarcastically.

Or perhaps, selfishly.

But it's not about me. Not at all.

It's still a shock, though, and maybe because this news is so unexpected, I need to ask the next question. "Did Ian know?"

Kana nods sadly. "Yes. He knew. We were the only ones who knew. He didn't want to say anything to anyone until I was far enough along, until we knew that everything was going to be okay."

Her voice breaks, because he's not the one who gets to share this news.

I look away briefly, blinking, then back at her. The woman who holds a piece of Ian inside her. It's humbling and awesome. She's growing a person, and that person is a part of my brother and a part of her.

I drag a hand through my hair, questions still racing. "I didn't realize he was able to. After the chemo treatments."

She laughs. "We thought that too. We were both surprised. But his last chemo was nearly a year before he passed, and that's why it was entirely possible."

Holland clears her throat and pipes in, "For men, the chemo kills the sperm, but the body restarts making it again in time."

Kana nods. "Yes, that's what my doctor said too, after I realized I was late. We think it happened on Ian's last trip here in late February."

That was before the cancer fully returned with a vengeance in March. Talk about the nick of time. "You guys were like Indiana Jones grabbing his hat before the stone wall came down."

"Yes, I suppose we were," she says, and the conversation ceases as the waiter returns with the drinks.

"How did he take the news?" I ask once the waiter's gone.

"He took it well. He was sad but happy, if that makes sense. I told him in person."

I tilt my head, grasping for when she might have seen him. "I thought that was his last trip."

"I flew to Los Angeles. Do you remember?"

"It was when I was in Miami. I wasn't able to meet you," I say, a little wistfully.

She nods. "Yes. I saw him and told him then."

I scrub a hand over my jaw. I never thought twice about her visit. It never occurred to me how important it was. It was simply a trip—her last trip.

But it was so much more.

"I came to town to tell him," she adds, filling in more gaps. "I couldn't give him that kind of news on the phone or over Skype. I needed him to know in person, so I visited him, and we went out and celebrated with a game of bowling."

Like a bright flash of neon at night, the last puzzle piece slides perfectly into place.

Everything that mattered to Ian lay on the table in a neat pile—my parents' last words, the reconciliation with Laini, the news of his child.

But wait.

No. That's not possible.

"Ian didn't come back. He didn't leave the magnet in the pile," I say slowly, taking my time with each word.

She swallows and pushes a strand of hair from her face then takes a sip of the drink. "I left it there," she says quietly, when she sets down the glass. "I wanted it to be with the other memories. It was my memento of the last time I saw him."

Next to me, Holland's shoulders shake, and she wipes a finger under her eye.

A lump rises in my throat, and I swallow roughly. "I can see him celebrating at a bowling alley. I love that you were able to."

"We talked about when to tell you. We didn't want to say anything right away, in case it didn't work out. I told him I would wait as long as I could before I told you. He wanted that too."

"Why?"

She takes a breath. "He didn't want you to face any more loss if you didn't have to."

That was my brother. Always looking out for me. "I get it. You don't have to apologize for keeping it to yourself. I completely understand," I tell her, and the thing is—I do.

There was a time when I wouldn't have. But that time has passed. I'm not the guy who clipped a car for no reason. I'm someone who tries to understand.

"I was twelve weeks pregnant at his memorial service. He didn't want me to travel. He didn't want anything to happen to the baby. So I stayed home. I stayed here. It broke my heart not to go," she says, her voice stripped bare. She stops, swipes at her cheek, and Holland grabs a napkin from the table and hands it to her.

Kana thanks her and dabs at her eyes.

"But he gave me something when I was in California. He asked me to bring it back here and hold on to it so I could give it to you once I told you about the baby. I didn't know then, of course, that you'd be in Tokyo, so I planned to send it to you. Now I can give it to you myself. I don't know what it says."

My spine straightens. "For me?" I ask, the words feeling foreign on my tongue.

Kana dips her hand into her purse and takes out an envelope. She gives it to me. "It's sealed."

I regard it like a precious artifact with terrifying and beautiful powers.

I try to steady my breath. Try to keep my shit together. Holland rubs my back, a soothing gesture.

I stare at the envelope for several seconds, maybe a minute. I don't know how I won't fall to pieces when I read this letter that comes from beyond the grave.

But I don't know if it matters whether I fall apart or not.

I'm here with the women in my life—the one I love, and the one who is the mother of my brother's child.

I slide my finger under the flap.

36

Hey Andrew,

If you're reading this letter . . .

Wait, hold on . . .

Cue: laugh track . . .

I mean, c'mon. How awesome is it to say that? It's like something you'd see in a movie, all foreboding and whatnot. How many times can you truly say, "if you're reading this letter?" Maybe . . . once.

But seriously, if you're reading this letter, it means one thing: I knocked up a woman.

Who knew the boys could still swim that far? But hey, I suppose I've got strong swimmers.

It also means I need you.

This is the truly serious part. This letter is for you. No one else has read it. No one else has seen it. You need to know this because you're the only one who can help me now.

I'm not here, but you are, and that's why this falls on your shoulders.

I need you to take care of my kid.

No, I don't mean raise the kid. Please. Go live your life.

What I mean is this: please make sure Kana is taken care of. Please make sure our baby is too. In late April, I opened a new mutual fund. You might have found it when going through my financials and wondered what it was about. You might not have gotten there yet. In any case, you will, because it's part of what I left behind.

You'll find all the paperwork for it if you go to my accountant's and get the info. It's the new one, nicknamed "tadpole." Clever, huh?

You're in charge of my stuff, and I need you to look out for my family. My family includes you, but it also includes two new people.

I'm asking you this from beyond the grave because I know you'll do it. Because this matters to me. Because you're my brother, and I love you so damn much. You used to say I looked out for you, and maybe that's true.

But Andrew, I need you now. I need you to look out for me.

P.S. Try not to miss me too much!

P.P.S. If you ever make it to Tokyo, there are some pictures I took of Holland one of the days the three of us hung out. I put them behind a photo frame. I wanted you to have them. You know, on account of you being irrevo-

cably in love with her. I took them to remind you that you really ought to find a way to get back together with her.

Look at me, telling you what to do from the next life.

Well, I have to sign off now. But in case I haven't said it enough, I love you, in this world and the next one.

Ian

37

Andrew

We exit the subway at Shibuya Station, where we began our trip here more than a month ago. That out-of-time feeling returns, like I'm a little bit lost again.

But that's only because his letter—his news—was so unexpected.

"I can't quite grasp it," I tell Holland as we head down the escalator. "There's a part of him that's still here on earth."

She squeezes my fingers. "It's intense to think about. It's humbling."

I nod. "That's it. That's exactly it. And it's wild too." I look at her and smile. "Like he had the last word."

She laughs. "This is one helluva last word."

Talking about the news—the baby, holy smokes, the baby—with Holland helps me process the enormity of what's to come. Actually, talking with her has helped me with so many things, since way back when.

"Hey," I say, stopping outside the Hachiko mosaic and pulling her close.

She tilts her head in question. "Hey, what?"

I run my fingers through her hair. "I like talking with you. That's all."

She dusts a quick kiss on my lips. "I like talking with you too."

We turn, and I tap the mosaic dog's head, then she does the same.

When we reach the crossing, I gently grab her wrist. "I want to take a picture."

"Be my guest."

"Of both of us."

"I've been wanting that photo for a long time."

We stand in front of the intersection, and I lift the phone and snap a selfie. I send it to her.

Andrew: We don't have to miss each other anymore. We can have each other.

After she reads it, she takes my hand and we walk home.

* * *

I pick up the Lucite frame for the first time since the night I arrived. I turn it around and slide the photos out from the back.

"I can't believe I ever thought anything else of these, even for a second," I say as Holland looks at the pictures with me.

"You didn't, Andrew." Her voice is soft, reassuring.

"What do you mean?"

She taps my heart. "You knew. You knew in here. You just weren't ready to fully understand everything he'd done. But what else could they be but for you?"

"You think I always knew?"

She nods. "Sometimes we know the truth, but we can't face it for whatever reason."

I wrap an arm around her and tug her close. Sandy lies at our feet, watching.

"Do you remember this day?" I ask, showing her the picture of her hair blowing in the breeze, her gaze trained on the lens.

She studies the shot of herself near a cherry blossom tree, and soon a smile forms. "I think that's the day we went to the Imperial Gardens. The cherry blossoms were beautiful."

I turn to the next shot, the one of her outside the pachinko parlor.

"That was later the same day. It was cold at night, so I changed my outfit. And then we sang karaoke."

I place the photos on the table and bring her close, wrapping both arms tightly around her. "We should do karaoke again."

"So you can serenade me with Rick Astley?"

"Rick Astley, Ed Sheeran. Whatever it takes, Holland. I will do whatever it takes to keep you."

"You have me, Andrew."

"But I want to keep earning you, every day."

She smiles and leans her head back, looking up at me. "Just keep being you."

"I will." I drop a kiss to her forehead, thinking again how lucky I am for this second chance with her. "It's funny how Ian was trying to play matchmaker from the grave."

She sighs softly, snuggling closer. "You beat him to it though. You had me back before he sent you his directive."

"I didn't need to be told that twice. I needed you back. I wanted you back."

I tug her up from the couch and take her to bed, where I show her all the ways I plan to keep her happy.

Happy with me.

EPILOGUE

Four months later

Holland and Kana take me out to dinner to celebrate.

My firm landed its first international client.

One of Jeremy's investment start-ups is located here and needed an American lawyer. My buddy really is a rock star kind of friend.

I still haven't taken the Bar yet—that hell awaits me in a few more months, but I'm working closely with the other attorneys in Los Angeles, helping this start-up with its business needs here.

"Just a few more months and I can file some lawsuits and stir things up," I say as I raise a glass of sake.

Holland tips her cup to mine. "Or slap up some personal injury billboards at Shibuya Crossing."

But we both know I'll do neither. I like my simple life.

Kana lifts her water glass to toast. "To the soon-to-be newest lawyer in the Peterson family," she says, then winces, setting a hand on her enormous belly. Hats off to her—I've no clue how she can be comfortable doing anything, even eating a meal.

"Is it a contraction?" Holland asks, on alert.

"I'm not sure."

Kana breathes out hard then winces once more, until she smiles again. "Probably just Braxton Hicks. Let's keep eating. It'll take my mind off it."

"Let's pig out, then," Holland says, but she watches her like a hawk the rest of the meal and insists on sharing a cab home with her.

"I'm fine. I'm fine," Kana says as we drop her off.

"Call me if they increase in frequency. I'll go with you to the hospital," Holland says.

"My mom can help too," Kana says, since her family lives on the outskirts of Tokyo. She has parents and a sister, and they're all excited to welcome the newest family member.

So am I. I can't wait to meet my niece or nephew.

The next day when my class ends, Holland is waiting for me outside the door, ready to burst.

She grabs my hand. "Kana went into labor in the middle of the night. She had the baby! Let's go!"

* * *

Thirty minutes later, I'm walking into the hospital room to meet my brother's daughter.

Emotion wells up inside me as I cross the threshold. This is a moment I'll want to remember for all time. This is the stuff that matters, the people we write letters for. This little person will change the course of lives.

Kana looks exhausted but ecstatic, holding her baby in the hospital bed. The tiny person in her arms is gorgeous, with a shock of black hair and a scrunched-up face. "Her name is Anna."

"That's a beautiful name for a beautiful girl," I say reverently.

"Her full name is Anna Miyoshi Peterson," she adds, and my throat hitches. Over the first name, my mother's, and the last name too.

I look away briefly. "That's perfect."

"Do you want to hold her?"

I nod. "I do."

I take Anna and hold her, and I can't stop looking at this creation, who's part her mom and part her dad.

I still don't know if I believe in God or religion, but at that moment, I decide I do believe in something greater, something truer, something bigger than my brother.

I believe in this world.

I believe in hope.

I believe that love is stronger than death.

I don't know that Ian is watching over his infant daughter, but I know this—*I am*.

And I will.

I know something else, something that will be true her whole entire life. I lean in close to my little niece, making sure she hears me, making certain she knows. "Your daddy loves you so much."

I kiss her forehead, feeling his presence, and at last understanding him completely.

* * *

We leave and I take Holland's hand.

"She's adorable," Holland says, squeezing my fingers. "I think I'm in love with her already."

"She's easy to fall in love with."

"She feels like my niece too. Is it weird that I think that?"

I laugh. "No, it's not weird at all." Then I stop laughing.

The time is right, because sometimes it just is. Sometimes you have to grab the opportunity to let the ones you love know how much you love them. "But what if she became your niece officially?"

Holland stops in her tracks and shoots me a curious look. "Andrew . . ."

"Holland . . ." The ball is in my court, so I bring her close, cup her cheeks. "Want to go ring shopping so we can get married?"

She laughs, incredulous. "For real?"

I nod. "As if there's any other ending to our story but that. I'm marrying you, and you're going to be mine forever. Are you okay with that?"

I'm not nervous. I'm not worried. We are an inevitability. We are the sun and the moon and the stars.

She smiles. "I'm more than okay with that."

More than okay. Yeah, I'd say the same for myself. I found a way through, and now I'm living and loving with everything I have. I'm much more than okay.

I'm whole again.

THE END

Thank you for reading UNBREAK MY HEART! This book is a little different than my usual fun, sexy, sweet contemporary romances, and I'm so delighted that you took a chance on it! I'd love to hear what you thought! Feel free to drop me an email at lauren-blakelybooks@gmail.com and be sure to sign up for my newsletter to receive an alert when my next **books are available!**

Coming next is ONCE UPON A REAL GOOD TIME, a fun, sexy, swoony rock star romance

releasing in September! Chapter One follows and you can order it on most retailers!

Mackenzie

I'm not checking him out.

I am solely focused on answering the next trivia question. The game emcee spouts it out for the four teams vying for the prize at The Grouchy Owl bar. The prize being bragging rights.

The hostess clears her throat, brings the mic to her mouth, and asks the question: "Which Las Vegas hotel did the bachelor party stay at—"

I'm perched forward in the chair whispering the

answer to my teammate—*Caesars, Caesars, Caesars*—so we can write it on the answer slip before the hostess even finishes.

"—in the 2009 movie *The Hangover*?"

"So easy," I say to Roxy as she smacks my palm and mouths *ringer* while filling in the answer.

I'm not a ringer.

I was simply fed a steady diet of Trivial Pursuit, trivia books, and endless facts about the world as a kid.

That's all.

Also, I love trivia. Trivia helped me through some tough times as an adult, and by tough, I mean anxiety-ridden, sleepless, and stressful. That kind of tough.

As the hostess flips her cards to the next question, the guy on stage—the one I'm not at all checking out—adjusts the amp for his guitar. The Grouchy Owl has a little bit of everything—from darts, to pub quizzes, to pool, to live music from local bands. It's like a Vegas hotel right here in the West Village. Big Ike doesn't want patrons to leave, so she makes sure the entertainment options are plentiful.

And if that handsome hottie stays on the stage, I won't want to head home for a long, long time. Except I'll have to. I'm Cinderella, and I turn into a pumpkin in minutes.

But for now . . . *Hello, nice view.*

As the guy turns the knob on the amp, his brown

hair flops over his eyes. He flicks it off his forehead with a quick snap then runs his fingers down the strings on his guitar. Those fingers fly.

I bet they'd fly other places too.

Come to think of it, I better give him a full and proper appraisal, especially since the *Jeopardy!*-style theme clock blasting from the hostess's phone is counting down the seconds till we've all penned an answer to her latest question, which means I have time to ogle.

A thin blue T-shirt reveals inked and toned arms, and stubble covers his jaw—deliberate stubble. Not the I-didn't-shave-today stubble, but a healthy amount of scruff. Yum.

"Would you like your camera to take a picture, or have you captured Guitar Hero in your brain for posterity?"

I jerk my gaze back to Roxy.

Note to self: develop some subtlety when ogling. Especially since you're out of practice on . . . everything.

I flip a strand of hair off my shoulder. "I wasn't checking him out."

Roxy rolls her hazel eyes. "I'm hereby awarding you a trophy for the most unconvincing attempt at denial ever."

I huff. "Fine. He's crazy handsome. Look at those cheekbones. Those lips. Those eyes."

She sings his praises too. "Those hands, that ass, those legs."

I swat her arm. "Stop perving on my eye candy."

My best friend smiles wickedly. "It's so easy to see through you."

"I didn't deny it for long." I hold up one finger. "For, like, one round of denial."

She reaches for my iced tea and hands it to me. "Speaking of rounds, take a drink. It'll make you strong for the final round of the game."

"Sometimes I think you use me for the useless facts in my head."

"You don't have to think it. You know I do."

"Love you too."

"Also," she says, leaning closer, "your eye candy was checking you out as well."

My eyebrows shoot into my hairline. "Lying liar who lies."

The hostess taps the mic from her spot in front of Mr. Guitar Hero. "And now, for the final question in The Tuesday Night Grouchy Owl Pub Quiz . . ."

Like synchronized swimmers, Roxy and I straighten our shoulders in unison. I grab the pencil. Hold it tight. This isn't a first-to-the-bell game, but there's something about being on high alert that feels right. I'm ready.

Questions zip through my brain, answers following instantly as my mind exercises itself. *The Beatles were first the Quarrymen; at sixty-three, Jupiter has the most moons; the Pacific is 8,000 meters deep.*

"Which Whitney Houston song is an anagram of 'mention mine to me'?"

What the what?

I turn to Roxy, and we are matching slack-jawed, WTH memes. Admittedly, pop music is my weakest category, but I can handle the basic questions surrounding the genre. This question is a little left of center though. I try my best to cycle through the diva's tunes. We mouth to each other the big Whitney hits: "I Will Always Love You." "Greatest Love of All." "How Will I Know."

I shake my head, and Roxy furrows her brow.

I stare off at the stage when the guy with the surfer hair catches my gaze and mouths *hi*, startling me. Is he talking to me? Oh yes, he is, since he follows that *hi* with four more words.

Holy smokes.

He slipped me the answer.

I'm officially in love.

I grab Roxy's arm. "'One Moment in Time,'" I whisper, and I unleash a smile at Guitar Hero. Because we're one step closer to winning, and that's one of my favorite things to do on a Tuesday night during my hour-long escape at The Grouchy Owl.

But wait. How does hottie know a Whitney Houston song? Straight men can know Whitney tunes, right?

Of course they can. God, I hope so. He looks seriously straight. He's staring at me like a man who enjoys boobs stares at a woman who has them.

I sneak another peek. His fingers slide down the guitar as he tunes it. He raises an eyebrow and locks eyes with me, his lips curving up.

My stupid stomach has the audacity to swoop.

Of course, in my stomach's defense, the loop-de-loop makes complete sense. Not only is he a babe registering easily at 15.5 on the only-goes-to-ten babe-o-meter, but he's holding a guitar. The way he wields the Stratocaster cranks my libido up high.

That might be due to said libido's sadly solo life these days.

As the hostess collects the answer slips, Roxy nudges my shoulder. "Go talk to him."

I roll my eyes.

"Oh please. You can do it," she adds.

"I'm not going to go talk to some random guy onstage at a bar, prepping for his set."

"Why not?"

"Because," I sputter. "Because it's dangerous, risky, crazy, and I have a thirteen-year-old at home."

"Isn't Kyle out right now? Practice or something?"

"Yes, but I need to pick him up in a few minutes, and that means I should go."

Roxy pouts. "Don't go before we find out if we win. And don't go before you talk to Mr. Steamy McMusic."

I laugh and shake my head. "You go talk to him."

"I can't. He has your eye marks all over him."

"Good. I own the view."

I stand, and Roxy joins me to give a quick goodbye hug. "Love ya," I say.

"Thanks for coming out to play. It's nice to see your face every now and then."

I head to the door, nearly bumping into the curly-haired Big Ike on the way.

"Hey, Mack. Is Kyle ready for Pine Notes?" she barks.

"Starts tomorrow. He's so excited." As the keeper of all musical knowledge in the tristate area, she recommended the music camp my son's attending starting tomorrow, and it sounds like a fantastic opportunity.

"The teachers there are great. He's going to love it."

I give a thumbs-up, wave goodbye, and don't even bother to check and see if Mr. Guitar Hero is watching me, though I'm tempted.

I head down the street then turn the corner, hoofing it a few blocks to the community center where Kyle practices with some of the other kids his age. He's formed an ad hoc sort of string quartet with some friends in the city who like the same music as he does. Shortly after I arrive, the kids stream outside, and I smile at my little blond-haired, brown-eyed guy.

Okay, he's not so little anymore.

But he's still my guy.

"Hey, monster," I say. "How was practice?"

He slings his violin case over his shoulder. "It was good. We worked on a new Brahms concerto that's totally dope."

"That's the only way Brahms concertos should be."

During the short walk home, Kyle regales me with details of the music. His voice rises as he grows more excited, then he smiles at me, the metal in his braces occupying most of the real estate on his teeth.

We reach our building and go inside.

"Did you win big tonight?" he asks once we're in our apartment.

I shrug and smile. "Don't know. But we fought valiantly. Are you hungry? Want me to cook some scrambled eggs with rosemary country potatoes?"

He pats his flat belly on his trim frame. "I'm still stuffed from the sandwich you made earlier."

I gesture to his room. "Big day tomorrow. Go put your violin away and get ready for bed. We're leaving to take you to camp at seven thirty sharp."

He salutes me on the way to his room.

A few minutes later, Kyle has brushed his teeth, washed his face, and is reading his biography of Mariano Rivera. I park myself on the edge of his twin bed and knock on the book's spine. "Good guy or bad guy?"

Kyle only reads books about sports stars if he

deems them good guys, so I know the answer, but I ask anyway because I like knowing what's in his head. For now, since he hasn't hit puberty with a vengeance, he usually tells me what's on his mind. "Definitely a good guy. He's also the greatest closer of all time."

I'm not even a sports fan, but I know that. "Six hundred fifty career saves isn't too shabby."

"You're such a dork."

"From one to another." I tap his forehead. "Did you take your headache meds?"

He gives me a thumbs-up.

"Good." I give him a kiss and say good night. "Love you so much."

"Love you too, Mom."

When I retreat to my room, I find a message from Roxy on my phone.

Roxy: We won, but it was by the hair of our chinny-chin-chins! It was super close—we need to be tighter next time. Also, all this could be yours.

The screen fills with an image and tingles zip down my body. Damn, that man is dangerously handsome, especially with the intensity in his eyes as he plays that instrument.

I sigh happily. I'm so checking him out.

What's the harm? He's likely in some band that's making a one-night-only appearance at The Grouchy Owl, like many of the bands that play there do. I'll probably never see him again. Unless you count later tonight in my dreams. Because that face and those hands are definitely fodder for a good night fantasy.

Besides, fantasies are the only times I've had any action lately, and by lately, I mean years.

You can find UPON A REAL GOOD TIME here!!

ACKNOWLEDGMENTS

Thank you to Michelle Wolfson. Without her wizardry, belief and tenacity, this book would not be in your hands. Abiding gratitude to Lauren Clarke, Jen McCoy, Helen Williams, Kim Bias, Marion Archer, Virginia, Lynn, Karen, Tiffany, Janice, Stephanie and more for their eyes. Big thanks to Helen for the beautiful cover. I owe a debt of thanks to CD Reiss who helped me reshape this story into what it is now. Thank you to KP, Kelley and Candi.

ALSO BY LAUREN BLAKELY

FULL PACKAGE, the #1 New York Times Bestselling romantic comedy!

BIG ROCK, the hit New York Times Bestselling standalone romantic comedy!

MISTER O, also a New York Times Bestselling standalone romantic comedy!

WELL HUNG, a New York Times Bestselling standalone romantic comedy!

JOY RIDE, a USA Today Bestselling standalone romantic comedy!

HARD WOOD, a USA Today Bestselling standalone romantic comedy!

THE SEXY ONE, a New York Times Bestselling bestselling standalone romance!

THE HOT ONE, a USA Today Bestselling bestselling standalone romance!

THE KNOCKED UP PLAN, a multi-week USA Today and Amazon Charts Bestselling bestselling standalone romance!

MOST VALUABLE PLAYBOY, a sexy multi-week USA Today Bestselling sports romance, and MOST LIKELY TO SCORE, a sexy football romance!

THE V CARD, a USA Today Bestselling sinfully sexy romantic comedy!

WANDERLUST, a USA Today Bestselling contemporary romance!

COME AS YOU ARE, a Wall Street Journal and multi-week USA Today Bestselling contemporary romance!

PART-TIME LOVER, a multi-week USA Today Bestselling contemporary romance!

The New York Times and USA Today Bestselling Seductive Nights series including *Night After Night*, *After This Night*, and *One More Night*

And the two standalone romance novels in the Joy Delivered Duet, *Nights With Him* and Forbidden Nights, both New York Times and USA Today Bestsellers!

Sweet Sinful Nights, Sinful Desire, Sinful Longing and Sinful Love, the complete New York Times Bestselling high-heat romantic suspense series that spins off from Seductive Nights!

Playing With Her Heart, a USA Today bestseller, and a sexy Seductive Nights spin-off standalone! (Davis and Jill's romance)

21 Stolen Kisses, the USA Today Bestselling forbidden new adult romance!

Caught Up In Us, a New York Times and USA Today Bestseller! (Kat and Bryan's romance!)

Pretending He's Mine, a Barnes & Noble and iBooks Bestseller! (Reeve & Sutton's romance)

Trophy Husband, a New York Times and USA Today Bestseller! (Chris & McKenna's romance)

Far Too Tempting, the USA Today Bestselling standalone romance! (Matthew and Jane's romance)

Stars in Their Eyes, an iBooks bestseller! (William and Jess' romance)

My USA Today bestselling No Regrets series that includes

The Thrill of It (Meet Harley and Trey)

and its sequel

Every Second With You

My New York Times and USA Today Bestselling Fighting Fire series that includes

Burn For Me (Smith and Jamie's romance!)

Melt for Him (Megan and Becker's romance!)

and *Consumed by You* (Travis and Cara's romance!)

The Sapphire Affair series...

The Sapphire Affair

The Sapphire Heist

Out of Bounds

A New York Times Bestselling sexy sports romance

The Only One

A second chance love story!

Stud Finder

A sexy, flirty romance!

CONTACT

I love hearing from readers! You can find me on Twitter at LaurenBlakely3, Instagram at LaurenBlakelyBooks, Facebook at LaurenBlakelyBooks, or online at LaurenBlakely.com. You can also email me at laurenblakelybooks@gmail.com

95687557R00167

Made in the USA
Lexington, KY
11 August 2018